THE WALTONS

Times were hard in the Blue Ridge Mountains during the years of the Great Depression. For the seven Walton children, those years often meant doing without things they wanted, or making do with what they had.

All of the Waltons were forced to make difficult decisions which would shape their lives and the lives of the people around them—decisions which sometimes brought them into conflict with one another.

Sheltered by Walton's Mountain and sustained by the love of their parents and grandparents, the Walton children faced those decisions with courage and honesty and found time for joy and laughter which they would remember long after they had grown up.

OTHER BOOKS ABOUT THE WALTONS:

THE
WALTONS

THE BIRD DOG

BY DION HENDERSON
COVER BY MAXINE McCAFFREY

A WHITMAN BOOK
Western Publishing Company, Inc.
Racine, Wisconsin

PROLOGUE

"In those long-ago days of growing up on Walton's Mountain, everyone was very close, and that is what you remember first. There was the great warmth of shared affection, and the solid knowledge of the simple values that you learned from your parents—and from your grandparents, if you were very lucky. But there were private lives as well, and much of the growing up came, as it always comes, because of outside events that made it necessary for you to learn to apply your own values. Help was never more than a word away in those days, but in the end, the growing up was something you really had to do for yourself.

"There was a time like that one spring, when Mary Ellen was in the middle of her chicken project, and Jim-Bob found a friend of his own, and Grandpa remembered some more things that Grandma thought he'd forgotten."

[1]

GRANDPA SAID that after breakfast, he believed he'd take a trip into Rockfish and see whether the Baldwin dog had arrived on the night train. Jim-Bob almost choked, because he wanted to ask about the dog, but he had just taken a big bite of corn bread with a thick, dark slab of buckwheat honey on it, which is kind of messy to begin with, and if he tried to talk with his mouth full, someone would mention it. When you had a family as big as the Waltons', someone noticed just about everything, especially in the way of table manners.

So before he could swallow, Elizabeth spoke up, the way she usually did, with one of those silly questions that made you think it would be nice if little girls had to raise their hands before they talked.

"What's a dog doing on a train, Grandpa?"

"Why," John-Boy said, "I imagine he was sitting up there in the parlor car, reading a magazine and barking for dog biscuits every time the candy butcher came through."

Elizabeth stopped eating. "I never saw a dog do that."

Jim-Bob swallowed. "That's because you've never been on a train," he said scornfully.

"Neither have you," Elizabeth said. "Daddy, is John-Boy fooling me?"

"I'd have to say that it's possible he is," John Walton said. "At least, I never saw a dog reading a magazine on a train, and I've watched lots of trains pull in and out of town."

"Well, now," Grandpa said, "I don't recollect I ever saw that myself. But I surely have seen dogs sitting up in the parlor car. Bird dogs, riding right with their owners. I've even seen 'em riding in private compartments on trains."

Everybody at the long table looked at him.

"Not only that," Grandpa said, "but I've heard that years ago, when Mr. Lorillard took his dogs down to Georgia for the hunting, they traveled in his private railroad car."

Jim-Bob tried to imagine what it would be like riding in your own railroad car with your own bird dogs and going down to Georgia for the hunting. It was no use. He liked to watch the trains when they came through the village, but mostly he was interested in the engines, all black and trailing steam and making the cindered ground tremble frighteningly under your feet as they thundered past the old red station on their way to Charlottesville and beyond there, to Washington. He would have to ask Grandpa later about the private cars and especially about the dogs and the hunting. He tried never to forget anything Grandpa said about things like that, even though it seemed as if he would never be old enough to go hunting and the only dog they had was Reckless, who mostly hunted rabbits.

Grandma was talking now, anyway. "That's enough about bird dogs," she said. "I thought you'd forgotten all about those days."

"Now, Esther," Grandpa said, "there's some things a man never forgets. Like a quail dog that'll find the singles when a covey breaks up, a horse that can take a fence with a loose rein, a pretty girl—"

Grandma's eyes started showing little sparks.

"Especially," Grandpa said hastily, "when he's been married to her for fifty years."

"And a regular devil most of that time, old man." Grandma forgot about sputtering at him. "Anyway, it's time you forgot bird dogs!"

Mary Ellen said, "Doesn't anyone want to hear about my chickens?"

Olivia looked at her oldest daughter with mock despair. "I declare, honey," she said, "I don't know that we've heard about much else for the past couple of weeks."

"There's one thing," John Walton said. "That dozen eggs has lasted longer than any birthday present I can remember."

"They certainly lasted longer than any other dozen eggs around this family," Olivia said.

"Not much longer, though," Grandpa said. "After Old Sairy has been setting on those eggs about three weeks there won't be any more eggs."

Elizabeth was alarmed. "Why not?"

"Because they'll be a dozen little chickens instead," Mary Ellen said. "Genuine White Leghorn chickens. And then," she said triumphantly, "there'll be plenty of eggs. Genuine pedigreed White Leghorn chickens will lay an egg every day . . . pretty near every day."

"Only half of them," John-Boy said mysteriously. "The other half won't lay any eggs at all."

Mary Ellen looked horrified. "Why's that?"

"Because half of them will be hens, and half of them will be roosters."

"If you're lucky," Olivia said. "There might be more one than the other."

Mary Ellen said, "Mama, what will I do if they're all roosters?"

"Well, now," Grandpa said, "a genuine pedigreed White Leghorn rooster ain't all bad. You just take a big roasting pan—"

"Grandpa," Mary Ellen wailed, "these roosters are pedigreed!"

"Mighty tasty, all the same."

"You stop that, Zeb," Grandma said. "You've got the poor child worried to death."

"Well, we'll know soon enough," Olivia said. "They'll be chipping their way out of their shells before long."

Elizabeth asked, "How do they chip their way out of the shell?"

Jason had to get into the conversation, too. "Well, they have these big teeth, and when it's time to hatch, they just bite a big hole in the shell; then it breaks and there they are."

"That's about the way it is," Grandpa said.

"It is?" Jason was amazed. "I thought I was just fooling."

"No, sir." Grandpa explained. "A baby chick grows a regular little tooth—an egg tooth they call it—on its beak, and they do just like you say."

"I never saw any chicken with teeth," Jason said.

"They don't last long. But just before they hatch, if you listen to an egg real close, you can hear those little chicks going 'chip, chip, chip' against the inside of the shell with their egg teeth."

"Are Mary Ellen's chickens really pedigreed? I thought dogs were pedigreed," said Jim-Bob.

"Sure enough," Grandpa said. "But pedigreed dogs are mostly purebred. Having a pedigree just means you know who the folks and grandfolks are and what they were like, so's you know what the young ones are likely to turn out to be. I recollect a fellow I used to know claimed his pups were pedigreed—"

Grandma threw up her hands. "My land, we're back to bird dogs."

Elizabeth was thinking over what Grandpa said. "Say," she said happily, "that means *we're* all pedigreed, too."

After breakfast, Jim-Bob went outside, and Reckless came out from under the porch steps, yawning and stretching, because Jim-Bob generally saved a bite of ham or a piece of corn bread for him.

Jim-Bob said, "Are you a good dog?"

Reckless wagged his tail and hung his head modestly to indicate that he was. Jim-Bob held out the piece of ham, and Reckless took it quickly with an enormous snap that engulfed Jim-Bob's whole hand but did not touch him with a tooth.

Jim-Bob wiped his hand on his overalls. "Reckless, did you know that baby chickens have teeth?"

Reckless raised his ears so that his brow filled with wrinkles. He was a reddish hound, with a powerful curiosity, and clearly this business of chickens with teeth was news to him.

"Grandpa says you can hear them chipping away inside the eggshell," Jim-Bob said. "You got real good ears, Reckless. I'll bet you could

17

hear them easy. Couldn't you?"

Reckless was willing to concede this talent.

"I'll bet," Jim-Bob whispered, "if we went into the barn real quietly and sneaked up on the manger where Old Sairy is setting those eggs, we could hear the baby chicks chipping away inside the eggshells."

Jim-Bob moved toward the barn, Reckless at his side.

Old Sairy was what Grandma meant when she talked about the Old Cluck. That isn't necessarily what Grandpa meant when he said the same thing, but then he said that was just another term you learned in nature study that was useful in other connections. He mostly didn't say "Old Cluck" when Grandma was around. Anyway, Old Sairy was the best mother hen on Walton's Mountain. That didn't mean she was very agreeable otherwise. In the spring, when she got to feeling motherly, she'd scratch around and build nests and ruffle up her feathers and cluck busily to herself, and if she didn't have any eggs to sit on, she'd sit on those china eggs that you put in the henhouse to fool other hens into laying eggs like them. Grandma said that, in a pinch, Old Sairy would sit on doorknobs, so you'd as well give her a clutch of eggs to hatch. She liked being a setting hen so much that sometimes she didn't want to stop and wanted to keep it up all summer, and then Grandma would grab her and douse her in a pail of water, which restored her to the real world, all right, but didn't do much for her disposition.

But now, of course, she had a real clutch of eggs to set. She had her nest in the barn instead of the henhouse, where all the other hens were afraid of her. In the barn, there wasn't anything but the cow and the mule, except for some barn swallows that had put their nests up in the rafters. Even so, they had to put her nest in the manger down in the last stall, because if she was up at the front of the barn, she'd fly at Blue every time he moved, until he wouldn't even come into the barn.

So Jim-Bob and Reckless were pretty careful about going into the barn, and Jim-Bob stopped to rub Blue's soft nose and to scratch Chance's ears, talking to the cow in her box stall chewing her cud. That didn't fool Old Sairy. Boys and dogs were about her least favorite things, even at best, and now that she had a clutch of eggs, they were right up at the top of her list of things to worry about. She clucked suspiciously.

Old Sairy was a Rhode Island Red, and in the sun, she was a beautiful mahogany color, like an Irish setter—and just as shiny—but in the dark at the far end of the barn, she was almost invisible. Jim-Bob and Reckless could tell she was there, though, because the closer they got, the more aggravated were the noises Old Sairy made, until her clucking sounded a good deal like growling—and meant the same thing. But Jim-Bob really wanted to listen to the eggs, so he got a handful of scratch feed from the bag and held it out to Old Sairy, at the same time trying to reach under her, where she was all fluffed up covering the eggs beneath her in the hay.

But instead of taking any of the feed, she pecked his hand hard, and Jim-Bob yelled. This alarmed Reckless so that he barked, and Old Sairy lost her temper entirely. She came off the nest with her wings flapping, like an eagle after a lamb. Jim-Bob and Reckless got in each other's way getting out of the barn, with the old hen flapping and squawking furiously after them. Just as they got out the door, there was Mary Ellen coming in. She was almost worse than Old Sairy.

Mary Ellen was carrying a pan of fresh water,

and the first thing she did was to throw it at Jim-Bob. The second thing she did was to start yelling.

"Mamma Daddy Grandma," she yelled without pause for breath. "Jim-Bob is messing with my eggs!"

"I just wanted to listen to them," Jim-Bob said reasonably.

That made things worse. Reckless disappeared under the porch, and Mary Ellen yelled even louder and started after Jim-Bob, waving the empty pan, and Jim-Bob ran for the house. He ran right into Grandpa, who was coming out, along with everybody else, to see what the noise was, and Grandpa held off Mary Ellen with one hand and held on to Jim-Bob with the other and said, "Here, you young 'uns, what's going on out here?"

Mary Ellen wailed, "Jim-Bob was messing with my eggs!"

"I just wanted to listen to them," Jim-Bob said from behind Grandpa.

Old Sairy was standing at one side of the stoop with her wings bowed down and her neck stretched out, making threatening noises into the dark place where Reckless was hiding, and Mary Ellen was waving the empty pan and yelling, and everybody else was standing around looking upset.

"The plaintiffs all seem to have the best of it, so far," Grandpa said. "But you get an old hen all ruffled up, and she ain't nothing to reason with, and sometimes a young 'un ain't any better."

"Get along with you, old man," Grandma said.

"It appears to me," Grandpa said, "that you, Jim-Bob, would benefit from a certain amount of absence."

Jim-Bob peered around at Mary Ellen, who made an angry face at him.

"All right, then," Grandpa said. "How would you like to come along with me and see that Baldwin dog?"

"Yessir," Jim-Bob said thankfully. "I sure would."

[2]

THEY TOOK THE OLD TRUCK so Grandpa could deliver the Baldwin dog after they got it from the train. Ordinarily, Jim-Bob would have preferred the mule, riding ahead of Grandpa on Blue's ample back, but the truck was quicker. At least it would have been, if Grandpa had not driven so slowly, with the windows open so the spring air blew in their faces. "Plenty of time," Grandpa said, grinning at the way Jim-Bob fidgeted.

Above them, the flank of the mountain was white with dogwood, and the red dirt of the road was still wet and heavy, so the truck did not make much noise, except for the rattles when they hit a bump.

At Drusilla Pond, Grandpa stopped the truck and pointed out a fly hatch swarming above the young lily pads, with fish making dimples in the water beneath the flies. Grandpa said that one of these days they'd have to cut a good limber switch and he'd show Jim-Bob a thing or two about fly-fishing, because a man that was interested in bird dogs was certain to be interested in fly-fishing, too.

"Opens the door to a whole different class of entertainment," Grandpa said.

Jim-Bob said, "I know where there's a good stand of willow."

"I favor a lighter wood," Grandpa said, "one that's got more backbone. I've seen some real fancy fly rods in my time."

He was about to start the truck again, then stopped. "Hark!" he said. "Listen to the bob-white whistling."

Jim-Bob listened. "There's two of them. Are they talking to each other?"

"In a manner of speaking. I think the one up on the ridge is announcing that he's found about forty acres that's just about the right size for his family, and he'll take it kindly if other quail take note. Then the one that's down in the old buckwheat says that he don't have any interest to speak of in oak ridges, but that there buckwheat field is no more'n *his* family will be able to use when it hatches out."

"Is that what they're really saying?"

"Can't rightly say," Grandpa said. "What they're saying to *me,* now, is that there's going to be two nice coveys right handy here in the fall. That's the part that *I* hear."

Grandpa started the truck again, and there was a blur of red across the road ahead of them.

"Well," Grandpa said, "somebody else is listening, too. Fox out in daylight must mean there's a litter of hungry pups around somewhere."

"Will a fox eat quail?"

"If the quail aren't quick enough. But a nice tasty mouse would be better, and probably easier to catch. You want to remember, though, that when you're raising kids these days, you got to take what you can get."

"Yes, sir," Jim-Bob said. He did not see the advantage of a mouse over a quail when it came to eating.

The train was late. At first, Jim-Bob was afraid that they had spent so much time—lollygagging,

Grandma would have said—along the road that it had come and gone. But there were some milk cans and a box still waiting on the big iron-wheeled baggage wagon that stood on the wooden platform beside the tracks. The baggage wagon had a short tongue and a high bed so it could be wheeled up beside the baggage car and the baggage could be slid right over into the car without lifting.

There was a roof over the platform, and in the center of the porch, there was a bay window sticking out from the station building. The window had bars on it and a place where the station agent could lift a little gate and sell you a ticket, except Jim-Bob had never seen anybody buy a ticket. But even though the windows were very grimy, you could see the counter inside, where, besides the ticket box, there was a telegraph key, all bright brass, with a round black button on the lever that was used to send messages. There was another set, without a lever but with a Prince Albert tobacco can fastened to it, on the other side of the counter. That was where the messages came in, and the tobacco can made an amplifier so the telegrapher could hear the dots and dashes over the other noises around the station.

Jim-Bob knew what it was like inside: rough wood walls, all covered with ancient whitewash but still rough, with wood splinters that stuck up hairily, and benches worn very smooth, and a smell like the henhouse after Grandma washed it out with carbolic acid to kill the mites.

Grandpa stood looking south, down the tracks. There was nothing beyond the old red station except a chute and a couple of stock pens, with weeds growing in them, that Grandpa said hadn't been used since Jeb Stuart unloaded his cavalry there for a raid across the mountains toward Staunton.

Jim-Bob said, "Grandpa, is it true that if you put your ear down on the rails, you can hear a train coming long before you can see it?"

"I've so heard," Grandpa said. "Why don't you try it?"

Jim-Bob did. He listened hard, but he did not hear anything.

Grandpa looked down the tracks again and shook his head. Jim-Bob was still listening.

Grandpa said, "I've also heard that if you put a penny on the rail, when a train goes by, you'll double your money—in a manner of speaking." He took a penny out of his pocket and gave it to

27

Jim-Bob, who looked at it closely.

"What happens?"

"Well, the train wheels go over it and squash it out twice as big as it was. But then it's only half as thick, so it's not a clear thing whether a man ought to invest in it."

Jim-Bob thought of the people he could show it to.

"On the other hand," Grandpa said, "a penny will buy one of them big caramel suckers down at Ike Godsey's store."

Jim-Bob weighed the value of owning a curiosity against eating the sucker. Then he put the penny in his pocket. "Might try it with a bottle cap sometime," he said. "See if it works."

"A wise decision," Grandpa said.

Just then the agent came out of the station. "If you're waiting for the train, Mr. Walton, it'll be an hour or so. Big rainstorm last night down toward Lovingston, and they have to put a little more ballast on the roadbed."

"Well, sir"—Grandpa clapped a hand on Jim-Bob's shoulder—"we might go on over to Ike Godsey's and wait, mightn't we? That'll give you a chance to get rid of that penny before you change your mind."

Down at the store, Sheriff Bridges was talking to Ike, who was leaning on the counter under the picture of the N.R.A. Blue Eagle, and over in the side room, Yancey Tucker was shooting pool by himself.

"Now that Mr. Walton's here, maybe I can get myself a game," Yancey said.

Grandpa said, "Sweeten the pot, Yancey."

"How about a dime a game?"

"Can't hear you," Grandpa said. "Can't hear a thing."

Sheriff Bridges asked, "Dog come in, Mr. Walton?"

"Train's late."

"Dog?" Yancey Tucker put the six ball in the side pocket. "What kind of dog is it?"

"*She,*" Grandpa said, "not *it*. Bird dogs get referred to with some respect."

"Along with some harness horses and a few people," Yancey said. "I stand corrected. What kind of dog is she?"

"As I understand Harry Baldwin's letter to his aunts," Grandpa said, "she's a setter with a pedigree that goes clean back to Count Noble. She's been to see that Mohawk dog, and Harry Baldwin hopes she's in a family way. Which is why—"

Grandpa cleared his throat importantly—"I have been called in as a consultant while Harry's working up north this summer."

"You're the man for it, Mr. Walton," Ike Godsey said. "You've seen 'em all."

"I favor setters myself," Yancey Tucker said. "Nothing like a good Llewellin to get you a good mess of quail."

"It's all pointers now, though," Sheriff Bridges said, "except for the Mohawk dog. Since Mary Montrose and Becky Broom Hill and them big white dogs, it's been all pointers."

"I still favor setters," Yancey said stubbornly. "You got a good setter, and once he's trained, he's *trained*. But if you got a pointer, you got to go through the same blame thing every year."

"Setter's a lot more likely to turn into a self-hunter, if you don't watch out."

"I don't care," Yancey said, winking, "long as she takes me along. What's this dog's name, Mr. Walton?"

"Baldwin's something or other," Grandpa said.

"Knew a fellow up in Albemarle County," Yancey said, "had a dog named Taxes. Always wanted one myself."

Ike Godsey said, "Why in the world would you

want to call a dog something like that?"

Yancey grinned wickedly. "Just so's I could say, 'Every time I opened the screen door, in come Taxes.' "

"Any blamed dog would do that," Ike said.

"That's a joke," Grandpa said. "Income taxes. Get it, Ike?"

"Oh," said Ike.

Yancey banked the cue ball off the rail and sank the nine ball. "About the only income around nowadays comes from bank robbing . . . Clyde Barrow and those fellows." He winked again. "Except Mr. Walton, here. He picks up a quarter about every time he gets me into a pool game."

"Not hardly the same thing," Grandpa said, "as bank robbing. But my hearing's picking up. Did you say a quarter?"

"All right," Yancey said. "About as much a sure thing, though."

He racked up the balls again, while Grandpa selected a cue and squinted down it to make sure it was straight, then finally chalked it up. Jim-Bob put his penny on the counter, and without even straightening, Ike reached down and opened the glass and took out a big caramel sucker.

"That'll last all day, Jim-Bob," he said. "That's

why it's called an all-day sucker."

"If it don't, you bring it back," Yancey said.

Sheriff Bridges said, "I understand there's considerable income being made now and then with fighting chickens."

"Not around here, is there, sheriff?" Yancey seemed dismayed. "Why, chicken fighting is illegal in Jefferson County, ain't it?"

"It sure is," said Sheriff Bridges.

Grandpa said, "It seems to me I recollect that when I was young and sinful, I saw a chicken fight or two." He leaned over the pool table and set the cue ball smacking into the rack of balls. The three ball rolled very slowly toward the side pocket and finally dropped. "Looks like I got solids," he said, chalking smugly. "Yes, sir, I recollect a time down in Roanoke when there was a Red Pyle and a Duckwing Gray matched, and there must have been a thousand dollars change hands."

Jim-Bob said, "Who won?"

"As I recall, the Gray did," Grandpa said. "He was a shuffler. But he wouldn't have been no match for one of our Virginia hackles." Grandpa looked hard at Jim-Bob, as though he hadn't seen him recently. "Now, see here, young feller, you want to remember that when you're participating in conversation among gentlemen, you're liable to hear things that wouldn't really interest the ladies, should you think about mentioning them."

"Yes, sir," Jim-Bob said, his mouth full of sucker.

"Well," Sheriff Bridges said, "I certainly hope nobody in Jefferson County is raising any fighting chickens, Virginia hackles or whatever, or we'll be serving a lot of stewed chicken over to the jail. Mostly," he said grimly, "to the feller that was raising them."

"Why, nobody'd do a thing like that," Yancey said. "Especially not in Jefferson County."

He looked at the table, and Grandpa was drawing a bead on the last solid-colored ball.

"Say, Mr. Walton," Yancey said plaintively, "aren't you even going to give me a chance to get one shot in this game?"

"Not if I can help it," Grandpa said. He shot, and the seven ball dropped. "Now, where's that black scalawag, Yancey, and you'll owe me another quarter."

Suddenly Jim-Bob heard the distant whistle. "Train's coming," he shouted.

"Pshaw, boy"—Grandpa pretended to scowl—

33

"you almost made me miss that shot."

Yancey sighed. "But not quite. Here's your quarter, Mr. Walton."

"Many thanks for the exercise," Grandpa said. "Next time you break, Yancey. Right now, Jim-Bob and me have to go see about that dog."

Sheriff Bridges said, "Mind if I come along, Zeb? Kind of like to see a class dog again myself."

"Me, too," Yancey said.

"I got to stay here and mind the store," Ike Godsey said, "but you all stop on the way back and show me, y'hear?"

When they got back to the station, the train was just pulling out, but Jim-Bob hardly glanced at the chuffing locomotive, moving out ponderously, with black smoke coming out of its stack in explosive bursts. He ran on ahead and saw the baggage wagon on the platform, clear of milk cans and boxes now, with only a crate on it.

The crate was made of wood slats, with only a small space between so you couldn't really see inside. Jim-Bob clambered up, stepping on the spokes of the big iron wheels, and fumbled excitedly with the cover. He hardly noticed it wasn't fastened, until he had it open, and then he stood staring into the crate as though he couldn't believe his eyes. His mouth hung open.

Grandpa came up, a little excited himself, with Yancey and Sheriff Bridges.

"What's the matter, boy?" Grandpa said. "You afraid she's going to bite you?"

Jim-Bob shook his head. He looked as though he might cry. All he could do was point at the inside of the crate, and Grandpa pulled it over where he could see inside, himself. Then he turned and took a step after the train, but it was almost out of sight. Sheriff Bridges came over and looked in the crate and pursed his lips.

"What's the matter?" Yancey Tucker asked. "Somebody say something!"

"Not much to say," Sheriff Bridges said. "Crate's empty. Somebody stole her, or she got away. Anyway, the dog is gone."

[3]

EACH ONE OF THE MEN had to open the crate and see for himself that the dog was gone, and she certainly was. Then, for a few minutes, they all stood on the platform and looked down the tracks and across the fields, and Jim-Bob even looked up in the tree behind the station, knowing it was foolish but still not able to help himself. It seemed if they all looked hard enough, someone would be certain to see the dog standing somewhere, just waiting for them to look at her. The station agent finally came out and opened the crate and looked inside it, then looked accusingly at everybody, as though they might be hiding the dog, until he looked at Sheriff Bridges, who looked kind of accusing himself—after which the station agent helped Yancey look down the tracks.

"It ain't the railroad's responsibility," he said. "Somebody probably stole her. There's a lot of tramps around nowadays, trying to cheat the railroad out of their fares."

"Spare us the details of the railroad's revenue problems." Grandpa sounded a little brisk. "Right now I'm interested in a paying passenger who didn't get where she was supposed to get."

"Seems to me," Yancey said, "that a baggageman might have opened the crate to give her a drink, or something, and forgot to fasten it again, and she just jumped out."

"Well," the station agent said, "the train *was* stopped for a while down the line, while they fixed the track."

"Be easier to find her"—Sheriff Bridges was taking the professional view—"if a tramp took her. Plenty of dogs around, but not many tramps leading class setters."

"That's right," Yancey said. "A dog lost in the mountains may be lost a long time."

"There's a whole lot of forms to fill out," the station agent said unhappily. "Claims and all."

"I don't look forward to it," Grandpa said.

"I'll have to take them over to the Baldwin sisters and tell them about it. I don't look forward to it at all. Miss Mamie, in particular, was looking forward to running a puppy nursery this spring."

They loaded the crate into the truck. There was a note on the top that said, PLEASE WATER BUT DO NOT FEED. That was because a dog might get sick in the crate if it was fed, and, besides, you didn't know what they might feed it. And there was a plate on the end of the crate that said, BALDWIN'S MARY.

"That's a good name for a dog," Jim-Bob said.

"You bet," Grandpa told him. "Mary's a good setter name. Mohawk Pal's mother was named Mary—Mary Jepp—so you have to say it's a good setter name."

Jim-Bob had never heard of a dog named Mary, but he was glad to know it. Even if he never saw the dog, he knew her name, and somehow that was a comfort.

Grandpa drove the truck home without saying very much. You could tell by the grim expression on his face that he was thinking. Jim-Bob noticed that Yancey Tucker's roadster was catching up to them, and it turned in behind them.

John Walton and John-Boy were working at the sawmill, sawing railroad ties out of eight-foot oak logs. Jim-Bob waved and jumped out of the truck shouting, "The dog is gone!"

John Walton cupped his hand behind his ear to show that he couldn't quite hear what Jim-Bob was shouting, then went and turned off the noisy old engine that drove the saw.

"That's mighty strong language, Jim-Bob," his father said. "What is it that you're doggoning?"

Jim-Bob was mildly affronted. "I didn't dog-gone anything, Daddy. I said the dog was gone."

"Slick as a whistle," Grandpa said. "All that came in on the train was an empty crate. If, that is," he sniffed, "railroad agents are to believed, which I would recommend only under very limited circumstances."

Yancey Tucker was out of his car now and joined them. "Doggone dog," he said. "That's a good one, Jim-Bob."

"I've heard better," John Walton said. "Now, tell me what happened."

So Grandpa and Yancey told about how the train was late and how they waited, but not what they talked about, and Grandpa didn't say anything about winning a quarter. But they told about the crate being on the wagon and how Jim-Bob was the one who found out the dog was gone and how hardly anyone believed him at first, but had to go look for themselves. John Walton went over to the truck and looked, too, and John-Boy looked at the catch that was supposed to hold the crate closed but hadn't, for some reason. Grandpa said that Baldwin's Mary had probably gotten hungry or thirsty or both, and maybe scared, too, and when the train was stopped, she pushed the crate open and jumped off somewhere, although there was no telling where. Yancey Tucker leaned toward the notion that somebody riding on the train had opened the crate and let her out, and now he had himself a nice dog.

Grandma and Olivia Walton and Mary Ellen came out of the house, Grandma wiping her hands on her apron, and while they all stood talking, Jim-Bob found himself sort of edged out of the crowd, even though he'd been the one that found out the dog was gone.

Reckless came around the corner of the house, carrying an old bone and looking as though he wanted to find some place to hide it.

One of the barn doors was standing partly open, as it generally was, and Reckless stuck his head inside, sniffed calculatingly, and then went in. There was something he'd forgotten, though, and in about ten seconds he came sailing out of the barn again, with Old Sairy flapping her wings and squawking right behind him.

"Sure is a broody hen," Yancey Tucker said.

Mary Ellen started to yell as soon as she saw what was happening.

"Daddy, Reckless was after my eggs again!"

"He was not," Jim-Bob said. "I just saw him walk in there with a bone."

"Broodiest old hen in Jefferson County," Grandpa said. "Sit on doorknobs, be that all there was to sit on."

"He was so after my eggs," Mary Ellen yelled at Jim-Bob, "and it's all your fault!"

"Blamed nuisance," Grandma said. "Once she gets that clutch hatched out, I'm going to give her a good dousing."

Reckless was going so fast he missed the hole under the porch the first time around. He swung out around the truck, looking for help, with Old Sairy right behind him, flapping and squawking and even gaining some, so he didn't stop but kept right on going around, and this time he dived under the porch and went scrambling out of sight.

Old Sairy stood just at the edge, with her neck stretched out and her feathers ruffled up, making threatening noises.

Jim-Bob was watching Reckless and didn't see Mary Ellen coming after him until she grabbed him by his suspenders and started shaking.

"Every bit of it is your fault!" she yelled.

John Walton separated his two children.

"Whoa up, now," he told Mary Ellen. "Jim-Bob wasn't anywhere near that old hen, as we all saw."

"I know, Daddy," Mary Ellen said. "But he took Reckless in there the first time to look at the eggs, and now Reckless wants to eat them."

"Sure is a broody hen," Yancey Tucker said admiringly.

"He had a bone," Jim-Bob said, yelling a little himself. "I saw him."

"That's enough now, both of you," John Walton said.

Grandma said, "An egg-sucking dog is a caution."

"Only way to cure an egg-sucking dog is to give him a pepper egg," Yancey said.

Jim-Bob wanted to know how you did that.

"Well," Yancey said, "you take a regular egg,

and you make a little bitty hole in each end, and you blow the egg right out of the shell, without breaking it. Then you fill it up with red pepper and leave it in a nest or somewhere where he'll find it."

"Will that cure him?"

"I don't rightly know," Grandpa said, "but it'll purely spoil his taste for pepper, if not for eggs."

Over beside the steps, it appeared that Old Sairy had told Reckless about all she had in mind regarding miscellaneous dogs poking around her property. She walked slowly and with great dignity back toward the barn.

Grandma sniffed. "Walks like she weighs two hundred pounds. Wait'll I douse her."

"Don't do anything hasty," Yancey Tucker said. "Hen like that is hard to find."

"Sure is a broody hen," Grandpa said, with a wicked grin.

"That's a fact," Yancey said, as though he hadn't heard it before. "Now, Mary Ellen, I want you to tell me all about your chickens. I'll bet they're all going to be champions."

Just loud enough for Mary Ellen to hear, Jim-Bob said, "Roosters."

She looked at him balefully over her shoulder,

but she couldn't resist the chance to talk about her eggs. Anyway, Jim-Bob felt better. A man can stand only about so much abuse when he's innocent. He went in the back door to see if he could find a biscuit to share with Reckless, who'd been some put upon himself.

After supper, Grandpa said he was going to take the dog crate over to the Baldwins and break the news to Miss Emily and Miss Mamie. The Baldwin sisters lived in a splendid house with stables out back and hedged gardens on the side, but the whole thing looked a little run-down, because there hadn't been people around to take care of it very much since Judge Baldwin died, which was quite a while ago. The Dutch boxwood edging the red brick walks had bushed out until the walks were like the maze that used to be over beyond the gardens. Jim-Bob remembered it from getting lost there once when he was very small. The boxwood had grown unchecked, so that now it was a tangled thicket with no paths left at all. There was a pink locust blooming by the portico and a redbud standing by the old fountain and a few daffodils turning brown—but mostly there were weeds.

The Baldwin sisters were very understanding. "We certainly know it was no fault of yours, Mr. Walton," Miss Emily said. "Isn't that right, sister?"

"It certainly is," Miss Mamie said. "And we are so obliged to you for all the difficulties you have incurred in tryin' to be of service to us."

"It was my privilege, ladies," Grandpa said very formally. "And I want you to know I'll do everything in my power to help recover your dog."

"Harry will feel so bad," Miss Emily said. "He was *so* lookin' forward to raisin' a few quality puppies again."

"I must say," Miss Mamie contributed, "that I was anticipatin' that way of passin' the summer myself. I declare," she said prettily, "I've been sweepin' and cleanin' in the old kennel so that it's as clean as the kitchen."

"It hasn't looked like that since the Judge passed away," Miss Emily said. "Papa kept some quality dogs, you know, Mr. Walton."

"Indeed I do, ladies," Grandpa said. "It was my pleasure to accompany him on many an autumn afternoon, dealing, when good fortune would have it, with bobwhites."

"Those were splendid days. . . ." Miss Mamie took a lacy handkerchief from her sleeve and touched her eye. "I do believe, Mr. Walton, that it would not be out of place on this occasion to offer you a small glass of the Recipe, so that you may toast those vanished times."

Grandpa looked at Jim-Bob thoughtfully, and Jim-Bob looked at the breakfront, with all the little china dolls in it.

"I don't think it would be out of place at all," Grandpa said firmly.

"Then let us go into the Judge's study," Miss Emily said. "I think that would be most appropriate."

Judge Baldwin's study had a strong, pleasant, familiar smell, and Jim-Bob realized that it was like the smell in Ike Godsey's store, over in back where the harnesses and bridles hung on pegs in the wall. That was because there was so much leather in the room: the old law books, with gold lettering on tawny spines, the sofa with the hump on one end, and the big chair. There was a china closet with some faded rosettes and ribbons in it, some cups that were almost black with tarnish, and a rolltop desk. Above the desk was a big picture in a wide golden oak frame. The picture showed a big black setter looking right out at you, and in the background, a man with splendid moustaches stood proudly, with a shotgun across his chest. An engraved brass plate under the picture said: MAGISTRATE.

"I do believe he was the Judge's favorite," Miss Mamie said. "He was a Campbell dog."

"Papa was partial to the Tennessee dogs," Miss Emily said. "He believed any dog goin' back to Mr. Campbell's Fan was bound to have a certain nobility."

"Not that Virginia dogs don't have nobility," Miss Mamie said hastily.

"That is a point upon which I am not qualified to venture an opinion, ladies," Grandpa said, "being a man whose interest in quail dogs is related directly to a hot skillet."

"Of course," Miss Mamie said, "but the field trials were another world."

"Yes," Miss Emily said dreamily. "The balls, and the silver and crystal, and the young men so tall and handsome. . . ."

"Those days are all gone now, sister," Miss Mamie said briskly. "And they'll be gone for our dear nephew as well, if we are unable to recover Baldwin's Mary."

Jim-Bob asked politely, "Is Baldwin's Mary a Campbell dog?"

"No indeed," Miss Mamie said. "There have been no Campbell dogs in your time."

It looked as though Grandpa was going to say there hadn't been any in his time, either, but considering the implication that might have had for the Baldwin ladies, he thought better of it. Instead, he became very businesslike and told them about the claim forms and how they should write Harry Baldwin and ask him to send some pictures of Baldwin's Mary so that Sheriff Bridges could send them around and people would know what Baldwin's Mary looked like, in case they happened to see her.

After that, Grandpa had another glass of the Recipe because Miss Emily said dealing with all of these complicated matters must have made him thirsty, and he said now that she mentioned it, he believed it had. Jim-Bob had some cookies and milk, and then it was time to start for home.

It was dark by this time and turning chilly, and once Grandpa had to stop the truck because a possum was puttering along in the road, his skinny tail sort of curling around by itself behind him. Grandpa said something about if it were fall instead of spring, that confounded possum wouldn't be so smug.

Jim-Bob was getting sleepy, but he was thinking about the picture and the ribbons and the cups, and presently he asked, "Grandpa, how come you didn't go to the field trials, when you like bird dogs so well?"

"Well," Grandpa said, "it's a matter of obligations."

Jim-Bob was not sure what obligations meant.

"Well, sir," Grandpa said, "a man gets to make a number of choices in his life, and it seems like every time he makes a choice, he takes on some more obligations."

That did not seem to help much, and Grandpa turned his face so that, in the faint lights from the dashboard, Jim-Bob could see he was smiling.

"I guess you might say an obligation is something you know you ought to do but had rather not."

Jim-Bob was still thinking sleepily about that, when they turned in at home. Then suddenly he wasn't sleepy at all.

The lights all were on in the house, and somebody was running out beyond the barn with a lantern, and it was plain that something was wrong. Something had happened.

As soon as the truck stopped, Elizabeth came running out, waving her arms.

"Come quick, Grandpa," she said. "Reckless has broken all of Mary Ellen's pedigreed eggs."

[4]

IT TOOK QUITE A WHILE to find out what had happened, because everybody had a little different account of it and everybody wanted to tell his share. John Walton finally got the children shushed so he could tell Grandpa the main story, which was how they were all in the house listening to Fred Allen on the radio, when the ruckus started—in fact, the ruckus might have been going on for some time. Elizabeth heard it first, because she only listened hard to the show when Senator Claghorn was on, but she said she heard Reckless barking and chickens squawking and Chance mooing, and then Blue brayed, and everybody heard it and rushed outside.

By that time, it was dark, so they had to find

a lantern and light it, and Reckless was barking off in the woods somewhere, and occasionally they could hear Old Sairy squawking.

Anyway, they went into the barn and there, where the eggs had been in the nest, almost ready to hatch, there was nothing but a clutter of broken eggshells and a few red feathers. And, of course, Mary Ellen almost fainted, and now she was upstairs crying and wouldn't talk to anybody.

"She feels pretty bad, poor child," Olivia Walton said. "She was really looking forward to those chickens."

Jim-Bob said, "Reckless never did it."

"Now, son," John Walton said, "there's pretty strong evidence here."

"I'm inclined to agree with Jim-Bob," Grandpa said. "Old Sairy really had that dog buffaloed. I never saw him move as fast as he did this afternoon when he poked his nose into the barn and she took exception to it."

Reckless was still barking off in the darkness, and John Walton cupped his hands and called him, but Reckless was making so much noise he couldn't hear. Then Grandpa went into the barn and took the hunting horn down from its peg and blew a long, mellow note on it, and Reckless stopped right in the middle of a bay.

Just then John-Boy and Jason came back with Old Sairy. John-Boy had partly wrapped his jacket around her, but she was so upset she didn't even mind being carried. She looked sort of disheveled, with some feathers missing, and she sat in John-Boy's arms, blinking at the lantern light and clucking occasionally. She didn't even pay much attention when Reckless came back in response to the horn.

The hound was very excited, with his tongue hanging out and dripping from all the running and barking. Grandpa told him to sit, and he kind of bounced down a couple of times before he really was sitting, his tongue hanging out sideways.

"Naughty dog!" Olivia scolded.

Reckless suddenly retrieved his tongue and looked startled.

"Got no conscience," Grandma said. "Hasn't got enough common decency to look guilty. Just like a man."

Grandpa took Reckless by the muzzle and ran his finger far back along the roof of his mouth. Then he held his finger up for John Walton to see.

"No feathers," he said. "This dog hasn't been

handling any chickens lately."

"Could have panted them out," John Walton said. "Anyway, I think we'd better tie him up."

"Lock the barn door after the horse is stolen," Grandma said, although she said it pretty quietly.

"Now, Ma," John Walton said, "nobody had any idea that he was going to do a thing like this, after being around chickens all his life."

"It's all Jim-Bob's fault for taking him in there this morning," Elizabeth said.

Jim-Bob looked at her angrily, because they were supposed to be friends, being the two youngest in the family, but he had learned already that you couldn't always be too sure about girls.

"That's enough of that, Elizabeth," John Walton said. "Everybody feels bad enough without laying blame around. John-Boy, you put Old Sairy in the henhouse tonight so's she can get herself organized, and then tie up Reckless."

"It's time for everybody to get to bed now," Olivia said. "I'll go up and talk to Mary Ellen."

"No use crying over spilt milk," Grandma said.

"I know," Olivia said, patting Grandma's arm, "but that's a hard thing to learn when you're Mary Ellen's age."

Jim-Bob walked into the house all by himself,

but before he started up the steps, his father put a hand on his shoulder.

"I know you never meant to, son," John Walton said. "Even if your going out there this morning got Reckless interested in the eggs, I know you never meant to."

Jim-Bob nodded, because he thought that if he said anything, he might cry. He went upstairs, and in the girls' room he could hear his mother talking soothingly to Mary Ellen. But there was no sign it was making Mary Ellen feel better, unless just knowing someone felt sorry and cared about you was enough to make you feel better.

Thinking that made him think about Reckless. He waited until he was sure everyone was asleep; then he crept downstairs, found a biscuit in the bread box, and took it outside, where Reckless was sitting at the far end of his rope, looking despondently at the moon. Jim-Bob petted him, but Reckless continued looking at the moon.

"I'm sorry, Reckless," Jim-Bob whispered. "Elizabeth was right; it was all my fault. And I'll bet you didn't even do it."

Reckless finally was mollified. He turned his head and licked Jim-Bob's face. Then he ate the biscuit, and Jim-Bob crept back to bed, hoping

55

he did not wake anybody else. He was a little surprised to find that believing in somebody made you both feel better.

On the way home from school, Jim-Bob lagged behind the others until, by the time they passed Drusilla Pond, they were out of sight. Jim-Bob took off his shoes and stockings and waded out. The water was pleasantly chill on his warm legs, and soft sand squished up between his toes. He splashed along to where the trunk of an old hornbeam tree lay partly in the water, punky on top from all the years of being wet and dry again, despite how hard it was underneath, and climbed up to sit in the sun. A foolish young bullfrog, darkly brownish green, with the round marks like ears on his head so you could tell he wasn't a pickerel frog, jumped wildly from the place where he'd been sitting on the log, almost invisible against the dark wood and green moss. The water was so clear that Jim-Bob could see him streaking toward the soft bottom beyond the log, where the cattails began.

A bream darted at him threateningly, then returned quickly to the round nest it was protecting, where the silt had been fanned patiently away so that the eggs would rest on sand. The bream was in bright nuptial colors, its throat a vivid orange and the blue lines on its gill covers standing out like road maps. Jim-Bob watched it swim truculently around the little sandy nest, the moving fins fanning water over the precious eggs. A dragonfly alighted suddenly on the log, almost on Jim-Bob's foot, its double wings glistening with reds and greens and blues, although you could still see through them, then as abruptly darted away. A redwing blackbird popped out of the cattails, missed the dragonfly by a wide margin, and returned to its nest. Jim-Bob had seen a lot of blackbirds chase dragonflies, but he had never seen one make a catch.

Far beyond the ridge where the old Littlefield farm buildings, long unoccupied, stood in their orchard, a train whistled lonesomely. At once, almost as though it were answering the train, came a bobwhite's whistle, much closer.

The quail whistled again, and Jim-Bob thought it came from just beyond the pond, where the collapsing rail fence around the old buckwheat patch made a corner at the edge of the oak woods.

He put on his shoes and stockings and walked as carefully as he could through the boggy wire grass toward the fence corner. The whistle came again, and he was sure of the spot. It would be fine, he thought, if Reckless were here, especially if Reckless were a bird dog. He imagined himself standing there, holding his shotgun across his chest and saying, "Hie on there, Reckless!" and Reckless would sweep across the field unerringly and come to a sudden point at the fence corner. Except, of course, Reckless was not a bird dog and wouldn't point, and if he went across the field, he'd more than likely scare up a rabbit and go baying after him.

He was very close to the fence corner, where the rails had sort of leaned over into each other and the grass and blackberry vines had grown up among them in a tangle, and he hadn't heard any more.

Then suddenly there was a fluttering in the grass under the rails. Jim-Bob stopped and looked hard, and there was a quail hen almost close enough to pick up, her bright eyes watching him. One wing was stretched out to one side, and she turned her head to follow him whenever he moved, and when he reached down ever so gently to pick her up, she fluttered away a few feet and stopped again, watching him. He followed her again, trying to be even more careful, and the same thing happened. He was about to get down on his hands and knees, so he wouldn't frighten her, when a big male voice spoke up behind him.

"Whoa up there, boy," the voice said sternly. "You quit bullyraggin' that quail, you hear?"

Jim-Bob jumped up in alarm, and the quail suddenly burst from the grass and went sailing across the buckwheat field to the orchard.

"She was hurt," he said foolishly. "I was trying to help her."

"Didn't look hurt when she finally got you away from her nest, did she?"

"No, sir," Jim-Bob said. "Is that what she was trying to do?"

"Yes, it was," the man said. He was a tall old man, maybe even older than Grandpa, with moustaches like the man in the picture over Judge Baldwin's desk, except that his moustaches were white, and so was his dog, instead of black like the dog in the picture.

"By jingo," the old man said, "I've got a mind to send you home to tell your father that Jim Randolph told you to quit bullyraggin' settin' quail hens."

"Yes, sir," Jim-Bob said unhappily.

"By jingo," the old man said, "can't you say anything but 'Yes, sir'?"

"Yes, sir." Jim-Bob felt more foolish every minute. Then he said weakly, "I know Jingo was a pointer."

The old man looked at him hard, then took off his hat and brushed it with his hand. He brushed the sleeve of his jacket and the worn leather facing on his old whipcord pants and put the hat back on his head.

"That's a fact, boy," he said in quite a different tone. "Jingo was a pointer; he certainly was. What else do you know about him?"

"Well," Jim-Bob said, "he was the grandfather of Hard Cash, who was one of the two greatest prairie chicken dogs of all time."

"You know the other one?"

"Algonquin."

"Yes, sir, boy. Algonquin. And I'll tell you a true thing, boy: There never was a dog like Algonquin."

"Yes, sir," Jim-Bob said.

"We're back to that now," Mr. Randolph said. "Where you find out things like this, boy?"

"I listen a lot," Jim-Bob said. "And I read

Field & Stream down to Ike Godsey's store whenever I can. *American Field,* too."

"Well," Mr. Randolph said, "I guess in a case like this, maybe you'd like to see what that quail was protectin'."

"I sure would."

"You be careful now, and be sure you don't touch anything. But you look under that corner post, where the rails are kind of fallen down and the grass kind of comes together. See something?"

Jim-Bob leaned over very carefully, and within the clump of grass he saw a nest full of pure white eggs. He counted; there were sixteen.

"That'll make a real nice covey come fall," Mr. Randolph said, "if nobody robs the nest or scares her off, you hear?"

"I wouldn't do that," Jim-Bob said honestly.

"I believe you."

Mr. Randolph came out of the brush a little way, and his dog limped forward toward Jim-Bob, wagging her tail. She was a beautiful setter, nearly all white, except for her black ears and the tan markings on her face and front legs, but she was very dusty and one of the front legs was done up in a splint so that she could not step on it.

"Gee, she's hurt," Jim-Bob said. "Is it bad?"

"Bad enough," the old man said, "considering she's soon to have a litter. But we'll make out," he said to the dog, "won't we, Nell?"

The setter looked up at him and wagged her tail. Jim-Bob wanted to ask more about how she got hurt and about the complicated way the splint was rigged up, but he thought it wouldn't be polite.

"All right," Mr. Randolph said, a little more distantly. "Get along with you now, boy."

"Yes, sir," Jim-Bob said. "Shall I remember you to my father?"

"Might better not," Mr. Randolph said. "Nell and I come from away down below, and we'll be going on over the mountain right soon now."

"I might remember you to my grandfather," Jim-Bob said. "He's the one who knows about bird dogs."

"I reckon he's a fine man," Mr. Randolph said, "and you ain't really such a bad boy, after all. But there have been better days, boy, and maybe there will be again." He patted Nell's head absently. "No, sir, boy, I'd take it right kindly if you didn't mention meetin' me to your father or your grandfather or, for that matter, to anyone."

"Yes, sir," Jim-Bob said.

"Do I have your word on it, now?"

"Yes, sir."

"But don't forget about the quail."

"I won't," Jim-Bob said.

He walked back through the bog. When he got to the road that went past Drusilla Pond, he looked back, but the old man and the dog were gone.

Jim-Bob shook his head, puzzled, and started for the road, then remembered to go back and pick some of the blue flags blooming along the bank. He had saved half a sandwich from his lunch for Reckless, and he thought that if he brought some flowers home for Mary Ellen, she'd feel better about the eggs.

[5]

AT THE BREAKFAST TABLE on Saturday morning, Grandpa wanted some berry jam for his biscuits, and Erin went down to the fruit cellar to get some but couldn't find any. Olivia Walton shook her head and smiled and said Erin couldn't see her nose in front of her face, then went down herself. Pretty soon she came up again, looking sheepish, and said she guessed that the jam must be all gone, and Grandpa said it was a pity that a man in the twilight of his days couldn't have some berry jam for his biscuits.

"All *right*, old man," Grandma sputtered. "After breakfast, I'll pack us a lunch and we'll go up on the mountain by Granny Ketchum's old place and pick some wild strawberries."

"Not me," Grandpa said promptly. "Little bitty things. I'm more cut out fer handling twenty-foot field pine logs."

"It takes a hundred wild strawberries to fill a half-pint box," John-Boy said. "I read that in Mr. Jefferson's *Garden Book*."

"Two quarts would make a nice batch," Grandma said, "but I can fill in some with pie-plant."

Jason said, "Ben and I have to help Daddy and Grandpa at the sawmill."

Mary Ellen looked sideways at her mother.

"I'd rather pick strawberries than clean house," she said.

"Never mind." Grandma got up and went over to the big maple kitchen cabinet beside the sink. "You all remember how busy you were when it comes time to eat strawberry jam on hot bread. Jim-Bob and I'll pick 'em without any help."

"I'll help," Elizabeth said.

"Let's see," John-Boy said, "if Grandma and Jim-Bob can each pick two strawberries a minute, it'll take nearly four hours to pick two quarts. But Elizabeth can eat one a minute, so it may take you all day."

"I won't eat a single one," Elizabeth said at

once, then paused. "Well, maybe just one. But I'll pick two a minute, like everyone else, and put the other one in the box."

"And come home with a tummyache," Olivia said. "You'd better stick to the lunch Grandma is making."

"Thou shalt not muzzle the ox on the threshing floor," Grandpa said piously. "That's from Scripture, you know."

"I know where it's from," Grandma snapped, "but I'm surprised you do, old man."

Granny Ketchum's place was up on the shoulder of the mountain, about where the road ran out, except by that time, the road wasn't worth anything to begin with. Jim-Bob could remember going up there with Grandpa once, to fish for the bright speckled fish in Ketchum's Run. They weren't big enough to amount to much for eating, but Grandpa used to like to catch them. He only caught three or four that time and took them up to the cabin and gave them to Granny Ketchum, talking to her in the fancy way he talked to the Baldwin sisters. Granny Ketchum gave Grandpa some tonic out of a blue mason jar, and Grandpa said it got his blood to circulating fine, and Jim-Bob sat on the flat stone steps and ate a big piece of hoecake plastered with salted goose grease, which worried him some to look at but which tasted delicious. Once he and Ben had been sent to fetch Granny Ketchum when all the Littlefields came down with a fever at the same time and Doc Vance was gone, and she had come down and brewed strange things in kettles on the wood range, and whatever it was, they got better.

But just a year or two ago, another kind of fever swept across Walton's Mountain. It was the same fever that had killed Granny Ketchum's husband and her little girl thirty or forty years ago, before Granny knew about herbs and medicines.

This time, Granny had the medicines to cure the fever in other people, but she herself was eighty-four years old and not afraid to die. The rose, she said, did not complain when it wilted on the bush. It had to wither and die to make room for new blooms.

So one morning, just at daybreak, Granny Ketchum quietly passed away. She left a note telling John-Boy to keep Blue, her mule. John-Boy, she said, had a nice, firm way about him that animals responded to.

After that, the children were not allowed to go to Granny Ketchum's place by themselves, mostly because of the herbs she had growing in her garden, but the younger ones all thought it was because the cabin was haunted. Even if it was, Jim-Bob wouldn't have been afraid, because Granny Ketchum had never been anything but kind and gentle and helpful with the sick in her whole life, that he knew of.

"Some of her healing was a lot of bosh, of course," Grandma said while they were eating lunch. "But she was a good woman. She brought a good many babies into the world, and I can't deny she could brew up a tea that made the grippe a mite more bearable."

"Did she learn from the Indians?" Elizabeth asked.

"Land, no," said Grandma. "She wasn't *that* old. She knew some things that everybody used to know about taking care of babies and burns and fever and things like that, and then she knew some other things that maybe doctors know, and then she knew the rest, the bosh part, and maybe that came from the spells and superstitions that people used to believe in."

"What all did she know, Grandma?"

"Like putting a spider web across a cut to make it stop bleeding," Grandma said. "Or taking a little vinegar and honey for a cough; everybody knows that. But then she had some plants there in her herb garden that were real medicine, and—" Grandma looked at them warningly— "some say they weren't all good medicine. Because if you had rats bad, for instance, she could give you something, and you wouldn't see any more rats."

"Can we look at the garden, Grandma?" Elizabeth said.

"Well"—Grandma seemed resigned—"if I don't let you, you'll probably sneak up here sometime and get into all sorts of trouble. Put your hands in your pockets, both of you, and you can look in over the gate."

The herb garden had a fence around it, and in addition to the fence, it had an Osage orange hedge, and the hedge was dense as a brick wall and twice as thick. It had grown together across the gate, so you couldn't get in easily if you tried. Inside, there were mostly weeds, but there were some flowers, too.

"There's some foxglove getting ready to bloom," Grandma said. "Granny used that to

69

make something for folks with heart trouble. And some bee balm for stings, and some columbine that has seeds she made tea out of, for headaches. And that old hemlock tree in the middle was what she made her turpentine out of, for bad aches. Those are some of the good things."

"How about the bad things?" Jim-Bob asked.

"Well, there's some monkshood"—Grandma frowned at him—"and some squill, and never you mind, young man."

Elizabeth kept on pestering. "What were the bosh things, Grandma?"

Jim-Bob could tell Grandma was getting exasperated.

"Well, young lady, Granny used to hold that a good many of her medicines wouldn't work unless the moon was full, or dark, or somewhere in between. Or you had to take 'em at midnight, or you had to take something and bury it, and foolishness like that. Or"—she was really sparking now—"you had to mix it with white corn whiskey to make it twice as good."

Elizabeth wouldn't give up. "Was it better with whiskey, Grandma?"

Grandma looked at Elizabeth and stopped being exasperated.

"I wouldn't know, young lady. Some certain old fools of my acquaintance are partial to that point of view, I must admit, but I'd rather be sick, myself. Now," she said, "let's finish picking strawberries and get on home."

Jim-Bob was looking at something on the bare ground in the dooryard.

"Did you hear me, young man?" Grandma said sternly. "It's time to finish picking strawberries."

"Yes, ma'am," Jim-Bob said quickly.

He had lost a good deal of his interest in picking strawberries, after what he'd seen in the dust of the dooryard. What he'd seen were footprints and dog tracks, which somehow seemed strange, until he figured out that they were made by a dog walking on only three legs. Jim-Bob did not know of any other dog that walked on three legs, so the tracks just about had to belong to Mr. Randolph and Nell. But they should have been across the mountain by now, unless something had happened. Maybe Nell's leg was worse or Mr. Randolph was sick or something.

The first thing he did was open his mouth to call Grandma and tell her, because she could help if anyone could, and the second thing he did was to close his mouth again, because he had remembered.

He had promised Mr. Randolph not to mention meeting him to anyone, so he couldn't tell Grandma. He would have to find out for himself whether Mr. Randolph needed help, because that's what you had to do when you gave your word. So now he had a secret that he couldn't share with Grandma, or even Grandpa, and it was not a very comfortable feeling.

"I hope we finish picking pretty quick," Elizabeth said. "My tummy doesn't feel so good."

"Then the picking will go that much faster"— Grandma wasn't very sympathetic—"if you're picking and picking, instead of picking and eating every other berry."

[6]

AT HOME, Grandma had Mary Ellen and Erin together at the sink, taking the tops off what looked to be about a million little strawberries, while she bustled around boiling jelly jars to sterilize them and getting the pot ready to cook the jam. They were complaining, sometimes separately and sometimes together, so that it sounded as though they were singing a sad song, and every time they started a new complaint, Grandma would bang some kettles together or open the stove door with a clatter and throw in some more wood, and when she didn't have either thing handy to do, she snapped, "Hurry up, now; I want to get this jam cooking before supper."

"Why doesn't Elizabeth have to help?" Mary Ellen said. "All she did was eat strawberries."

"I *picked,*" Elizabeth said virtuously.

"We both worked hard all day," Erin wailed, "cleaning and washing and everything."

Their mother was rubbing furniture polish on the piano and listening.

"You poor things," she said, smiling.

"Hurry up," Grandma said, banging the lid down on the stove. "I want to get this jam cooking before supper."

But it didn't work out that way. Before the girls had cleaned even half a million tiny strawberries, there was the sound of a car outside, and it turned out to be Yancey Tucker's roadster.

"Never knew that man to visit just *after* a meal," Grandma said. "Got a nose for food like a turkey buzzard."

"Now, Grandma," Olivia said, "that isn't a very nice way to talk about my cooking."

"Isn't what I meant," Grandma said, "and you know it."

"Of course I do, Grandma, but it just seems so much nicer for me to think he's partial to my pork chops and your pie."

"If it makes you feel any better," Grandma

said. "You think he's really partial to my pie?"

"Why, certainly."

"Too bad," Grandma said. "I'm making bread pudding tonight."

They heard Yancey talking to the men outside, and then they came in, Yancey carrying a big box carefully. Grandpa got a footstool, and Yancey put the box gently on top of it.

John Walton was chuckling. "Yancey, here, was telling us a story about a fellow he knows whose wife is allergic to washboards."

"For land's sake," Grandma said, "how'd that happen?"

"Well, sir," Yancey said, "every time she thought about doing the wash, it made her sick."

"I know just how she felt," Olivia said, then added, "You're just in time for supper, Yancey."

"Is it that time of day already?" Yancey appeared to be amazed.

Olivia told Mary Ellen, "Put on another plate."

"Better put on another pork chop, too," Grandma said.

"Tell you what." Yancey looked at Grandma with a sunny smile. "I'll stay on one condition."

"What's that, Yancey?"

"If Miz Walton has made some of her great

bread pudding for dessert."

Grandma went back to rattling pots on the stove, but she was a lot quieter.

Yancey said, "What I really came for was to make a business deal with Mary Ellen."

Mary Ellen abandoned the strawberries instantly. "What kind of a business deal, Yancey?"

"I heard what happened to your clutch of pedigreed eggs, Mary Ellen, and I'm purely sorry."

Mary Ellen looked as though she might cry again, and Yancey said hastily, "So I thought I might just provide you with kind of a substitute." He shook his head sympathetically. "Not as good as what you had, but it might work out anyway, long as you got Old Sairy."

"What's so great about Old Sairy?"

"She's a mighty broody hen," Yancey said reverently. "Now, here's what you do."

He opened the box on the footstool and held it open so they could look inside. There was a thick layer of excelsior inside, and cardboard dividers that made a dozen little squares, and inside each square was an egg.

"You just take these eggs and let Old Sairy brood 'em, and when they hatch out, I'll help you take care of 'em, and when the little chicks are ready, we'll divide 'em between us."

"It's a deal," Mary Ellen said, almost yelling. "How will we divide them, Yancey?"

"Well," Yancey rubbed his chin. "It's sort of a gamble."

Olivia said disapprovingly, "I don't know, Yancey. We don't hold much with gambling here."

"You're going to have to forgive me for using a word like that," Yancey said apologetically. "It's just a manner of speaking."

Grandpa coughed but didn't say anything.

"I tell you what," Yancey said. "Let's say we'll let the good Lord decide how we'll divide them."

"That's better," Grandma said.

"Yessirree," Yancey said, "you get to keep all the pullets, and I'll keep the roosters."

This time Grandpa said, "Aha!"

"Can I, Mama?" Mary Ellen was clearly yelling this time. "Can I, Daddy?"

"Well, honey," Olivia said, "it sounds all right to me. You just have to remember that they might all be roosters."

"Yes," Mary Ellen said, smiling craftily, "but they might all be pullets, too."

"That's a— Well, that's a decision I'm willing

to leave in the hands of the good Lord," Yancey said piously.

Mary Ellen suddenly looked very serious and put both hands up to her face. "Yancey, what if Reckless breaks up the nest again?"

Jim-Bob said stubbornly, "Reckless didn't do it."

"I thought of that," Yancey said, "and it'll work, whatever done it the first time. We'll just start Old Sairy out in a little old coop, like you use later on when the chicks are hatched and you watch 'em out on the lawn, where they can get some sun and grass. Only we'll put it right there in the barn and put a nest box and the eggs in it and put Old Sairy in there where nothing can get to her."

"Sounds like it'll work," John Walton said.

"Sure," Yancey said cheerfully. "And that's where your end of the bargain comes in, Mary Ellen, because you'll have to be sure Old Sairy gets plenty to eat and drink while she's settin' on them eggs."

"All right, Mary Ellen," Olivia said. "The men have time to go out and get the coop ready while we get supper on."

Jim-Bob went out, too, but there were enough

to work on the coop without his helping. Reckless was sitting out at the end of his rope watching, and Jim-Bob sat beside him and scratched his ears while they both watched.

Presently the coop was finished. John-Boy went to the hen yard to get Old Sairy, who had recovered enough by this time that he had to throw his jacket over her and wrap her up to keep her from pecking him. When he came back, carrying the jacket with the furious noises coming out of it, Reckless crawled under the porch.

All Sunday morning, Jim-Bob thought about what he had to do in the afternoon, and it made the time go very slowly. First, of course, he had to get ready for church and then go to church. Sunday School seemed to last forever, until Jim-Bob almost wished he'd gone to church upstairs with the grown-ups, because, while he found the Reverend Hawthorne Dooley surpassingly dull under most circumstances, at least he might have gone to sleep there, unless Grandma noticed and jabbed him with her elbow. If he could sit with Grandpa, he was all right, as long as he didn't fall off the pew, because Grandpa didn't stay all that alert himself during Mr. Dooley's sermons, although he liked the hymn singing beforehand.

After church, things went slowly, too, because it was a nice day and everyone dawdled, talking to everybody else and saying what a nice day it was. Finally they were home, and the Baldwin sisters came for Sunday dinner, which ordinarily would have been fine, except they didn't talk much about Baldwin's Mary. Two or three times, Jim-Bob thought he'd bring up the subject politely, but he couldn't think of any way of doing it politely, so he paid attention to his chicken and gravy, even remembering, most of the time, to keep one hand in his lap.

Finally Grandpa asked if they'd heard anything, and Miss Mamie said they had a letter from Harry, and their nephew was coming down when he could.

"Meanwhile," Miss Mamie said, "Harry said that he was perfectly confident that Mr. Walton could look after the affair as well as he could himself."

"And Harry's a *very* competent man," Miss Emily said, looking at Grandpa, her hands kind of fluttering over her plate.

"I take that as a high compliment, ladies," Grandpa said, "and I want you to know I'll do my best to deserve his confidence."

About here was when Grandma had the coughing spell. Then Olivia changed the subject, but not until Miss Mamie said that what Harry really was disappointed about was not having the puppies by the Mohawk dog down here at home, where Mr. Walton would have been able to stop over regularly and advise on their upbringing.

"It certainly is a pity," Grandma said. "I know he was looking forward to it."

"He's a dear, sweet man," Miss Mamie said.

Grandma started to say something, but Olivia dropped her fork, and Grandma jumped up to get the dishcloth, so no one ever found out what she was going to say, which probably was just as well.

Then, after dinner, the Baldwin sisters went home, and the grown-ups rested in the parlor. John-Boy was up in his room reading, and Mary Ellen was out in the barn watching Old Sairy sitting contentedly on her new eggs in the coop with bars across the front. The other children set up the croquet set on the lawn, and Jason asked Jim-Bob if he wanted to play. Jim-Bob declined, which was all right, because it was more fun to have four playing, so you could play partners, than it was with five. Jason would have rather had Jim-Bob playing than Elizabeth, but Elizabeth always made a fuss if she couldn't play, and when she did, they could have the boys partners against the girls, which meant that he and Ben always beat Erin and Elizabeth, unless Grandpa came along and made them let the girls win once in a while.

Jim-Bob went in and changed his clothes without anyone asking him where he was going. Then he slipped out the back door and went into the woods, until he was far enough away to swing back onto the road that led to Granny Ketchum's place, because he had to find out for sure about the footprints of the dog walking on three legs and whether Mr. Randolph really hadn't gone over the mountain with Nell, after all. By this time, he wasn't sure anymore about the tracks in the dust of the dooryard, partly because he was hoping so hard that he was wrong. If it was another dog and another man, then the problem was solved, because then he could tell about it without going back on his word.

On the other hand, if it was Mr. Randolph and Nell, he didn't know what he'd do, except that if they were in trouble or hurt or something, he would have to ask if it was all right to get help.

But he thought it would be a good idea to find out who had made the footprints before he decided anything, and he certainly didn't want to walk right up to the door and knock, especially if it turned out not to be Mr. Randolph.

There were more buildings besides the cabin up there in the clearing, although the cabin was much the handsomest, even though it was very old. It was made out of squared logs, so that not only was the outside straight up and down, but also the logs were notched out on both sides and fitted snugly together for their whole width, so that there was hardly any need for chinking. It had a big chimney made out of creek rock and red clay, long ago baked as hard as stone from the heat inside, and it was deep and wide at the scotchback, above the throat, so you knew it would draw enough to pick the rug off the floor inside, if you knew anything about fireplaces. The cabin would be dark inside, though, because there were only two small windows. When it was built, window openings were covered mostly with pig bladders, because glass was hard to come by.

Then there was a small barn that was made out of logs, too, although not nearly so fancy, but the bottom part of it was tight when it was well chinked. One end of the bottom part was for tools, and the other end was for the cow and the mule, with a high sill to keep varmints out, although it must have been hard on the cow sometimes. The upper part of the barn, where they used to store the hay, was just made out of poles, without any chinking and with several inches open between the poles, so that the hay would dry under the roof but would still be ventilated.

Then there was a structure that Jim-Bob would not have known was a pigpen, except that he remembered Grandpa telling him about it. It was low, but it was made out of big logs with spaces between them, and two other big logs on each end, each pair of them making an X, with just enough space under the center of the X to push a pole through from one side to the other, holding the top down. It was a very simple but effective piece of engineering that someone thought up to keep bears from tearing open the pigpen at night and killing the pigs. Once the pole was through the two X logs, the more a bear pulled on it, the tighter it held together.

There was a springhouse, too, made out of well-fitted logs, and it looked as though it might have been used for more than storing milk once upon a time, because there was a fieldstone fireplace nearby and some pieces of broken bottles and some tubing, which even Jim-Bob knew indicated a moonshine still.

Ketchum's Run came down off the mountain, very fast and cold, and ran under the springhouse, but where it came out, it had picked up enormously in volume, from the other springs there in the stone clefts. Below the springhouse was a deep, swirling pool of dark water, and where the water flowed out of the pool, it became a big creek that went on down to join the river.

Jim-Bob was very careful about how he approached the clearing this time. Instead of coming up the road in plain sight, he swung back through the woods and kept the springhouse between him and the cabin. He waited there quite a while, but he didn't see anything. Once he thought he heard someone talking, but he couldn't be sure, and he couldn't see the front door.

He started climbing down the great shelving ledges of gray stone around the foaming pool, to where the footlog was below, but the rocks were wet and slippery, and just as he made the last step down, his foot landed on a wet part of the stone, and, with a yell, he went over backward into the rushing icy water.

It was so cold he gasped and got a noseful of water. Though he had learned to swim long ago in Drusilla Pond, this was not Drusilla Pond. The current rolled him over, and the last thing Jim-Bob remembered was the shape of a pine tree against the blue sky as the water closed over him.

[7]

THE BLUE SKY was still there when he opened his eyes, but instead of the pine tree, there was the silhouette of a man's head with white moustaches.

"You almost done yourself in, boy." Mr. Randolph's deep voice was soothing but a little shaky. "If Nell hadn't come tearing over here barking her head off, you'd have been feed for the fishes."

Jim-Bob struggled to sit up. His stomach sloshed a little, so he knew he had swallowed a lot of water, and his nose had that funny stuffy feeling, like when Jason or Ben ducked him in the pond before he was ready, but otherwise he felt all right.

"I pumped you out pretty good," said Mr.

Randolph. "Way you were thrashing around in there, I didn't know whether I was going to pull out a boy or a black bear, who probably wouldn't have appreciated it much."

"I appreciate it"—Jim-Bob managed a weak smile—"but I'm cold."

"Sure enough," Mr. Randolph said. "Let's get you down to the cabin and get those wet clothes off you."

In a little while, Jim-Bob was sitting in Granny Ketchum's big chair in front of a big fire, wrapped in a musty-smelling quilt, and his clothes were hanging out on chairs to dry. He had never been in the cabin before, and he peered around a little nervously. It probably looked just about the way Granny left it when she died—right in this very chair, no doubt. With only the two small windows and the fire for light, it was dark in the room, but Jim-Bob could see that, besides the table and chairs and the sink with a water bucket standing on it, there were a lot of shelves on the wall, with mason jars full of leaves and dried flowers and what looked like roots. Jim-Bob sat up on the very edge of the big chair.

"Now, boy"—Mr. Randolph sounded more stern—"suppose you tell me what you're nosing around here for. I saw you yesterday, picking strawberries with your grandma and your little sister, but we kept as quiet as mice in here all the time."

"I saw Nell's footprints in the yard," Jim-Bob said. "Only three-legged dog I know."

"Just so." Mr. Randolph shook his head. "I suppose you told everybody about it, right off."

"No, sir. But you said you were going across the mountains when I saw you before, and I wondered if something happened."

Mr. Randolph chuckled and sat down himself. He had a corncob pipe and took out a big jack-knife and whittled some fine shreds off a plug of dark, sweet-smelling tobacco. Then he took a splinter of kindling, lighted it in the fire, and then lighted his pipe.

"Something happened, all right." He was smiling at Jim-Bob through the smoke, so it couldn't have been anything bad. "Yessiree, something happened, all right, and Nell and me had to find a place to hole up for a while. It looked like this place hadn't been used for some time, and it also looked like it belonged to a healer of some kind."

"Yes, sir," Jim-Bob said. "Granny Ketchum. She died a while ago."

"Looks like she was a real medicine woman and not just a healer . . . all those medicines up there on the shelf."

"What's a healer?"

"Well," Mr. Randolph said, "I've heard of some up in the mountains. They don't need to use medicine, but they can stop blood, draw out fire from burns, and cure things like thrash, by praying and like that."

Jim-Bob wondered what Grandma would say about that. Part of it was what she called bosh, but she certainly wouldn't say that about praying. It was very complicated. Suddenly he remembered what they had been talking about.

"What happened to make you stay here?"

Mr. Randolph chuckled again. "Just listen," he said.

Nell was over in the darkest corner of the room, and Jim-Bob could see her moving around, because she was white. But then something else was moving around, and there were small noises and squeaks.

"Puppies!" he yelled, bouncing right out of the chair. "Nell had her puppies!"

"Sure enough did," Mr. Randolph said. "Kind of took us both by surprise. But we got five nice puppies, and they're fine."

"May I look at them?"

"I guess that'd be all right, if you're real easy about it. Some dogs don't like to have anybody mess with their puppies when they're little, but Nell seems to like you pretty well."

"I'm obliged to her," Jim-Bob said. He moved quietly over to the dark corner, and there was Nell, lying with the five puppies in kind of a box Mr. Randolph had made out of old boards. The box was so the puppies couldn't crawl around and get lost and cold. Then he had folded up one of Granny Ketchum's crocheted rugs and put it in the box and had taken the oilcloth off the table and put that on top of the rug.

"Wouldn't it be better to have them on the rug?"

"Nope," Mr. Randolph said. "That rug is there for insulation. It keeps any drafts from coming up through the floor cracks and like that. And the oilcloth is easy to keep clean. You got to keep puppies mighty clean if you want to keep them healthy. A real whelping box would be up on legs, with nothing inside but fresh paint and maybe some newspaper, but this'll do fine."

Jim-Bob leaned over to look at the puppies.

Nell lifted her head and looked at him thoughtfully, then her tail thumped on the oilcloth. The five fuzzy puppies were all busy.

"Are they all going to be white?"

"Not altogether," Mr. Randolph said. "Can't tell for sure yet, but I'd say three were going to look a lot like their mother, and the other two are going to be ticked some with black."

Jim-Bob said, "I'd sure like to play with them."

"They'd best get some bigger," Mr. Randolph said. "Get their eyes open." He paused a moment, rubbing his chin as though he had to make up his mind about something. "You can come back," he said finally, "as long as you don't tell anybody about it."

Jim-Bob said, "It has to be a secret?"

"I reckon so," Mr. Randolph sighed. "Folks don't take too much to a traveling man these days, and small wonder. Especially not when he stops traveling and moves into somebody else's house. Times are hard, boy."

"Yes, sir," Jim-Bob said politely. "I know. Lots of folks don't have very much."

"And they want to keep what little they have," Mr. Randolph said. "Can't say as I blame them."

Jim-Bob said, "My grandpa says that us Wal-

that need it."

"I'd like to meet your grandpa sometime," Mr.
Randolph said, "but not quite yet."

He opened the cabin door and looked out. "It's
getting on late, boy, and your clothes are as dry
as they're going to get. Time to skedaddle."

"But I can come back?"

"Yes," Mr. Randolph said. "You shouldn't,
but you can, if you really want to. But remember
not to mention it, or I might be sorry I fished
you out of that creek."

"I'll remember," Jim-Bob said. He thought he
might add that he knew something about obligations, but that might be sassy.

It turned out to be a week before he got back.
The next day at recess, Erin got excited because
G.W. told them that somebody had discovered
a new haunted house. Mary Ellen laughed at him,
and that made G.W. mad, and he told a pretty
bloodcurdling story about how people walking
along the road had started hearing strange cries
at night, and seeing spooky lights in the woods,
and even seeing a genuine ghostly white shape
that appeared and disappeared at times.

"Somebody's old white heifer," Mary Ellen said.

"It was not," G.W. said heatedly. "People have seen all those things, and they were real."

"I thought they were ghosts." Mary Ellen liked to tease him.

"They were!" G.W. was getting flustered. "Real ghosts!"

Elizabeth was listening, with her eyes getting wider and wider, and Jim-Bob could feel himself getting interested.

"So where is this haunted house?" asked Mary Ellen.

"Granny Ketchum's old place," G.W. said. "Where she died, and you know what kind of a spooky old woman she was."

"Bosh!" Elizabeth cried suddenly. "Jim-Bob and Grandma and me were up there picking strawberries just last Saturday, and we walked around the garden and looked at all the medicine plants and everything, and there weren't any ghosts."

"Granny Ketchum," Mary Ellen said with vast disdain. "She probably took care of you when you were a baby, and maybe your mama when she was a baby, and now you think she was really a spooky old woman."

"Well, gee," G.W. said, crestfallen, "that's what I heard. I didn't really say I saw any of the ghosts myself."

"But you were willing to let us believe it," Mary Ellen said. "Let's play baseball."

All afternoon in school, Jim-Bob thought about how nice it was to have sisters like Elizabeth and Mary Ellen, who said the right thing at the right time, and the feeling lasted until suppertime.

Then it went away all at once, because at the supper table, Elizabeth had to tell all about how G.W. said that Granny Ketchum's place was haunted.

"And what did you say?" John Walton asked.

"I said, 'Bosh!' " Elizabeth was getting a lot of use out of her new word, but this time it got her into trouble.

"That's pretty strong talk for a young lady," Olivia said disapprovingly.

Elizabeth was wounded. "I heard Grandma say it."

"That's different," Grandma said. "Do as I say, not as I do."

Grandpa said, "That's from Scriptures."

"It is not," Grandma said waspishly.

"Oh," Grandpa said, pretending to be corrected. "I must have just thought it was, because I've heard so many preachers say it."

"Old fool," Grandma snapped, but Grandpa just chuckled and winked at John Walton, who chuckled, too.

"Anyway," Mary Ellen said, "G.W. didn't even know what house it was. It might have been the Littlefield house, because that's empty now, too."

"Oh, bosh," Grandma said loudly. "Just because folks move out of a house doesn't mean it's haunted."

Elizabeth nudged her mother. "There!"

Olivia stifled a smile. She said, "Be still, honey."

Grandma said, "Anyway, probably just some tramp stopped in somewhere to get warm. A body's got to keep an eye on everything these days, the number of tramps there are around."

"Now, Ma," John Walton remonstrated, "just because a man's down on his luck and out on the road looking for work doesn't necessarily mean he's some kind of a thief."

"Precious few of them looking for work,

though," Grandma sniffed.

"There must be others like Arch Littlefield, Ma," John Walton said reasonably. "When they couldn't even pay the taxes and lost their place, Mrs. Littlefield took the kids down to stay with her sister in Richmond, and Arch went out looking for work. But that don't make him a tramp."

"I'm not talking about Arch Littlefield," Grandma said, as though it settled something. "But I think the children ought to stay together on the way home from school and be mighty careful about talking to strangers."

"That's always a good policy," Olivia agreed.

So it was Saturday before Jim-Bob got back to see the puppies. He got his chores done early and caught his mother in the kitchen while Grandma and Mary Ellen were upstairs making beds.

"All through?" Olivia said, pleased. "Why, that's fine, Jim-Bob. Now you can go out and play."

"Yes, ma'am," Jim-Bob said thankfully and dashed out the back door and into the woods, before anyone could think of something else for him to do.

●

Mr. Randolph seemed glad to see him, and so did Nell. Mr. Randolph said there'd been considerable changes in the past week, and he was right. The puppies had their eyes open and were toddling around bumping into each other, chewing sort of tentatively on whatever got in the way, even if it was somebody else's ear or tail. Another week, Mr. Randolph said, and they'd be getting outside. And by the time they were weaned, he said, he'd make a leather pad and start throwing it around and see which ones were interested in hunting for it. Setters came slow, Mr. Randolph said, and he wasn't a man to be rushing things, but you might as well start early finding out what you got, as long as it was all in fun.

Sometimes, he said, setters were more likely to be natural retrievers than pointers, but you had to be careful about letting them learn to retrieve. Getting out there and getting the bird when it fell was fine for a shooting dog, he said, but it wasn't always what you wanted with a class dog. If you had a class dog, he'd probably be owned by a man with spaniels at heel to do the retrieving, and if by some chance you were lucky to have a real field trial dog, then you certainly didn't want them retrieving or even thinking about anything except going on to the far horizon and finding all the birds in the world. Besides, he said, a dog that retrieved was hard to keep steady to shot, because when the gun sounded they wanted to go, and championship dogs had to stay steady as a rock in the presence of game.

"There's an awful lot for a dog to learn," Jim-Bob said.

"The best ones are born knowing it," Mr. Randolph said. "All a trainer can do is help them find it all out and learn how to put it to use. I've had puppies not much bigger than these who knew more about birds than I did."

"Have you known an awful lot of dogs?"

"Yes, boy." Mr. Randolph patted Jim-Bob kind of absently on the shoulder and looked at the boxful of puppies, not really seeing them. "I go back a long ways. I remember Sioux, and that was the greatest setter of all time. I was there the day Jim Avent put him down against the Lorillard shooting dogs for something like a thousand dollars a bird—and Jim maybe not having a dollar in his pocket to pay if he'd lost—but he went home rich. Why, boy"—he took off his hat and brushed his coat—"I go clean back to Count Noble, that Mr. Sanborn brought over from Mr.

Llewellin's place in England. When he died, they had him mounted, and you can still see him in a museum in Pittsburgh." Mr. Randolph put his hat back on. "Of course," he said, "Dave Sanborn didn't own him then."

Jim-Bob said, "Is Nell a class dog?"

"You bet your boots," Mr. Randolph said. "And you're going to get a chance to see for yourself, because I think we can take her splint off today and let her walk on four legs again."

Nell seemed very worried while Mr. Randolph was unwrapping her leg. Jim-Bob petted her, and she licked Mr. Randolph's hand and worried some more while he felt the leg very carefully.

"It didn't heal too well." He was very disappointed. "I'm purely sorry, Nell, but it was a bad break, and I didn't have much to work with. Come on now," he said, standing up. "Let's try it out."

But Nell didn't want to try it out. She followed him but still walked without her leg touching the ground.

"Does it hurt?" Jim-Bob asked.

"I don't think so," Mr. Randolph said. "I think it's most likely habit. I had a dog got a toe caught in a screen door once, and it was sore as the dickens for about a week. But for years afterward, he'd limp on that foot when he thought of it."

He scratched his head thoughtfully, then snapped his fingers. "By jingo," he said. "I bet this'll work. Take her outside, boy, way down by the barn, and make her sit."

Jim-Bob did as he was told, with Nell limping cheerfully along beside him. Then they waited for quite a while, until suddenly they heard a puppy yelping. Nell's ears came up, and in an instant she was dashing for the cabin, running on all four legs.

Mr. Randolph came out smiling. "I hope that youngster forgives me for getting his ear nipped," he said, "but I reckon I can explain it was worth it."

After that everyone felt fine, and Nell capered around the yard, wanting to play, although she still limped when she was only walking. Jim-Bob wondered if they could take her for a walk.

"We'll start kind of slow," Mr. Randolph said, "but maybe next time you come back, she'll be ready to show you something."

[8]

JIM-BOB WANTED TO FINISH his chores extra early the next Saturday, but there were complications. He had done everything but bring in fresh bedding from the straw stack for Chance and Blue, but Jason and Ben were fooling around instead of cleaning out the stalls, which had to be done first. Jim-Bob left the wheelbarrow full of straw standing in the barnyard and went up into the loft to do the very last thing on his list of chores, which was to pitch down some fresh hay. When he came down, Jason and Ben were throwing straw at each other and yelling, and the wheelbarrow was empty, but the stalls still weren't cleaned.

They didn't pay any attention to Jim-Bob telling them to please hurry up, and presently he lost his temper and started picking up clods in the barnyard to throw at them, and his aim was pretty good. When he hit Jason on the ear, they forgot about fighting with each other and both chased Jim-Bob. They were just about to stand him in the rain barrel, Jim-Bob kicking and crying with rage, when John Walton walked around the corner of the barn and took in the situation, so it turned out all right.

"All right now, boys," he said in the quiet way he had, "party's over for a spell. Jim-Bob, you go along and find something interesting to do the rest of the day, and we'll just let your warlike brothers take it out on doing their chores, and yours, too."

Jason and Ben said together, "Gee whiz, Daddy, we were only fooling."

"I know," John Walton said. "But you were supposed to be working. Get along with you."

Jim-Bob didn't need a second invitation. He dodged into the kitchen to see about some lunch. Grandma was just taking a couple of big beef bones out of a pot, where she'd been boiling them for soup.

"Can I have them for Reckless, Grandma?"

"I suppose so," Grandma said, "but I declare, I don't know where that dog puts everything. The more you feed him, the skinnier he gets, and him doing nothing but sitting out there at the end of his rope, thinking bad thoughts about everybody."

"Not everybody; just Mary Ellen," Jim-Bob said. But he grabbed the bones and went outside, and that's what Reckless was doing, except you couldn't tell what he was thinking, exactly.

"Reckless," Jim-Bob said, "I brought you a bone. But you understand I have to save one, too."

Reckless looked at the bone sadly, as though from far away.

"Go on, take it," Jim-Bob said. "I promise I'm going to get you out of this somehow."

Reckless considered this offer of counsel at some length. Then he sniffed the bone, and finally, with a sigh, he took it and crawled under the porch. Jim-Bob tucked the other one under his shirt and dashed into the woods.

Mr. Randolph was pleased about the bone. He said it was just the thing for the puppies, to wear down their little needle teeth, which, he said,

Nell was getting less enthusiastic about every day, and he was glad it was good and boiled out. Some folks figured, he said, that it didn't do any harm to give puppies a raw beef knuckle to worry, but he didn't believe in letting them get used to the taste of it. Time would come, he said, when you might want a shooting dog to retrieve a bird that had been shot up some, and there was no use giving him a chance ahead of time to find out that he liked the taste. A class dog, he said, wouldn't disturb a feather on a wounded bird, and he couldn't abide a hardmouthed setter, although a setter wasn't as likely to be hardmouthed as a pointer.

When the pups were fully occupied with the bone, Mr. Randolph said, "Now then, boy, are you ready to see something?"

Jim-Bob was, so they walked through the clearing and into the woods and on up to the ridge, where the woods thinned out. There was a big meadow that went on, bowl-shaped, with a brushy little creek in the middle, until there was another ridge at the horizon.

"Don't want to put her into birds just yet," Mr. Randolph said. "Just like to see her move out, and this looks to be about as much a barren field as any. I've walked through here two, three times without seeing any bird sign, which I'd expect, because the birds all ought to be over yonder where there's some oak and an old field of cowpeas."

Then Mr. Randolph walked out a little way, with Nell close behind him, keeping her head almost against his left knee and still limping when she walked, and made her sit. He knelt in front of her, not touching her.

"I want you to go, Nell," he said softly, "I want you to go, girl, *go*."

Nell stopped looking around and looked straight at Mr. Randolph, and a light seemed to come up in her eyes as he talked to her, and then suddenly he stood up and touched the back of her head with his fingertips and said in a great voice, "Hie on!"

Nell went down the slope into the meadow grass, running so fast Jim-Bob couldn't believe it, straight as an arrow and swift as the wind for two hundred yards, and then, bending slowly, a white streak burning across the mixed green and brown of the field, sweeping it like some tremendous scythe, taking the wind and cutting the long meadow as if with a white-hot knife. And then, just at the creek, she changed direction so quickly that Jim-Bob thought she had fallen, but she had turned to the side and moved ahead, not running now but with a quick, decisive marching step, and then suddenly she stopped, with all four legs braced. Her head and tail raised slowly—and she froze.

Jim-Bob stood looking at her, unable to say a word, the cold chills chasing up and down his back.

"Lordy, lordy," Mr. Randolph said. "She's got as much style as Skyrocket. I don't care if she's pointing a possum."

Jim-Bob couldn't say anything at all. Mr. Randolph started down the slope, saying "Lordy, lordy," under his breath, and Jim-Bob followed. It took quite a while for them to reach Nell, and she stayed there staunchly as Mr. Randolph, sweating and puffing some, walked up beside her and gently patted her side, then walked on past her into the little tangle of brush she was pointing. For a moment nothing happened, and then there was a blur of red on the other side of the thicket, and a fox jumped across the creek, white-tipped red tail in the air, and fled across the meadow grass.

Mr. Randolph stood with his hands on his hips, watching.

"Pshaw!" he said, and you could tell from his face and the way he walked just how he felt. He went back toward Nell, and just before he reached her, he kicked unhappily at a clump of elderberry canes, and a quail exploded out of the middle of them, almost frightening Jim-Bob to death, but Nell didn't move.

"By jingo," Mr. Randolph shouted, "there *was* a bird here, after all."

He bent over and searched in the grass and said he didn't know how he'd missed the nest, but the chicks were all hatched out now and probably scurrying all around them, and a quail chick could hide on a pool table if it wanted to. Anyway, the fox was gone, so they'd be all right, and it was time to go back to the cabin, because enough was enough, the first time out.

Then he looked at Jim-Bob and said, "Cat got your tongue, boy?"

"Yes, sir," Jim-Bob gulped. "I mean, no, sir."

"First time you see it is a great time," Mr. Randolph said. "Myself, I saw Gladstone, and I couldn't talk for a week."

"Yes, sir," Jim-Bob said.

"There's nothing like a pointing dog, boy, except maybe lightning across a clear sky or thunder in the morning."

"Yes, sir," Jim-Bob said dumbly. But even feeling the way he did, he knew there was something in the back of his mind, and when the chills stopped running up and down his spine, he would get it sorted out and do something about it, because when he saw the fox running from the quail nest, he thought he knew what had happened to Mary Ellen's birthday eggs.

But as it turned out, when he got home, not even Mary Ellen would have been interested in the old eggs, because the new clutch that Yancey Tucker had brought were hatched out. Yancey was there, too, and about as excited as Mary Ellen was, and Mary Ellen was running all over the house and outside and through the barn and over to the sawmill, yelling that everybody should see her chickens.

"Shucks," Jason said, "they look just like ordinary little fuzzy yellow chickens."

"Well, they're not," Mary Ellen yelled. "They're genuine, pedigreed *special* chickens. Aren't they, Yancey?"

"You bet," Yancey said, and then, in case

Grandma was within hearing, said, "Excuse me, but they certainly are."

"I'd be willing to concede that." Grandpa was taking this all in, his thumbs hooked under the suspenders on his overalls. "Yes, I believe I would."

Yancey tried hard not to pay any attention.

Mary Ellen was peering into the coop, where Old Sairy had her wings spread and was clucking contentedly to her new family, with only an occasional warning to all the people gathered around.

"There must be nine of them hatched," Mary Ellen said. "I think there's only three eggs left."

"That's probably gonna be all there is to it," Yancey said. "Now, about the day after tomorrow, partner, you really have to go to work."

"Good," Mary Ellen said. "What do I have to do?"

"Well," Yancey said, "we have to move this old coop out on the lawn, where the chicks can get out and pick up grass and bugs and things like that but still can get back in the coop with Old Sairy if they get cold. And you have to remember to cover the coop every night, so it doesn't get too damp in there, and not to uncover it in the morning until the dew is off the grass, because getting wet is the worst thing that can happen to a little chicken."

"That's not hard," Mary Ellen said.

"But the main thing is to see that they always have plenty of fresh, clean water to drink."

"And should I give them chicken feed, like the other chickens get?"

"Sure," Yancey said. "But you got to remember, little chickens are pretty ignorant. They don't even know how to drink until Old Sairy shows them, and the same goes for eating. They'd as soon eat a pebble as a piece of wheat, until they learn better." Yancey rubbed his chin thoughtfully. "And then," he said, "a little later on, I know where I can get some good water-ground mash with all the good old vitamins still in 'er, and you can give 'em some of that with a little warm milk on it. And I'll show you how to make some corn bread that you can soak in beef gravy. They really like that."

"Gee." Mary Ellen was trying to remember everything Yancey told her. "I didn't know raising chickens was so complicated."

"It isn't," Grandpa said mischievously, "with ordinary chickens. But didn't you hear Yancey say these were very special chickens?"

"Of course," Mary Ellen said. "But I hope I do everything right."

"You'll do just fine," Yancey said. "And remember, all the pullets in this batch are yours."

"I will, Yancey," Mary Ellen said. "How long will it be before we can tell?"

"Oh, five or six weeks," Yancey said. "Maybe a little longer."

"About the same time," Grandpa said, "that you can tell the Law Grays from the Jungle Reds."

Grandma was just coming into the barn. "What's that, old man?"

"Nothing . . . not a thing," Grandpa said. "I was just offering an observation to the business people, here."

"Seems to me," Grandma said snappily, "that you could offer more help than your observations."

"Wouldn't think of it," Grandpa said. "Builds character to let Mary Ellen take on this here responsibility. And besides," he said to Yancey as Grandma moved out of earshot, "I want it clearly understood that I didn't have anything to do with this transaction—nothing whatever."

Yancey looked at Jim-Bob apologetically and rubbed his chin again. Then he said finally, "Might be just as well, too, to keep that old dog tied up for a little while."

"Reckless didn't do anything," Jim-Bob said. "He wouldn't touch a chicken, and I'll bet I can prove it."

"I'll bet you'll do it, too," Grandpa said. "But just to be on the safe side, let's leave Reckless tied up for a few days."

Jim-Bob turned around and left the barn. He stopped beside the porch, where the rope disappeared into the hole under the steps. "I will, too," he said into the hole.

But there was no response. All he could see was a hopeless and unstirring tail.

[9]

MR. RANDOLPH WAS UNEASY; he said so himself. Jim-Bob was sitting on the cabin floor, and the pups were all over him, chewing on his pants legs and pulling his shoelaces when they weren't chewing on each other, which some of them were most of the time. Every once in a while, Nell would come over to inspect the squirming pile, and a puppy would see her and charge, and she would retreat hastily out of reach.

"I'm purely uneasy," Mr. Randolph said again, pulling on his moustaches. "I don't reckon I can stay here much longer, and I sure don't look forward to going on down the road with five puppies to look after."

Jim-Bob hadn't thought about that. "Why can't you just stay here?"

"Well, now," Mr. Randolph said, "this here's a haunted house, isn't it, boy? That's one reason nobody has bothered us much—that and the fact that we can see anybody coming on the road for quite a distance. But somehow there ain't much really ghostlike about six dogs barking and my spare shirt and underdrawers flapping on the clothesline, and one of these days the sheriff is going to stop in and inquire just how I was related to Granny Ketchum, that I've taken over her property."

Jim-Bob was getting uneasy, too.

"On the other hand," Mr. Randolph said, "we been getting on pretty well here, Nell and me; eating real good. I got me some flour, although it's most gone, and a feller who was up on the ridge one night with a jacklight shared some deer meat with me—not that he knew he did—and left a mess of bones for boiling, and there's been plenty of greens in the garden, and I've got right friendly with an old cow that comes poking around now and then, so we've done all right. But now each one of them pups is going to start eating for himself, and the sooner the better, the way they're tormenting Nell. On top of that, they're going to need some shots for the distemper pretty quick, and I don't know what all."

Jim-Bob said, "Couldn't you sell them?"

"I been meditating on that," Mr. Randolph said. "That's what I figured to do, right from the first. But you know that Nell is a real *class* dog, and the two puppies that don't look just like her are carrying the same kind of black ticking that Mr. Feagin's dog had, the one that was National Champion back in 'twenty-eight and 'thirty. It just don't seem right to take puppies like that and sell them for meat dogs to folks who don't know that a pointing dog is something to uplift the spirit of man and make him hear music, instead of just to help some hunter fill the stew pot."

Mr. Randolph stopped pulling his moustaches and blew his nose.

Jim-Bob had an inspiration. "Maybe you could sell all the puppies to Harry Baldwin," he said.

Mr. Randolph did not seem very hopeful. "Who is Harry Baldwin?"

"Harry Baldwin is the nephew of the Baldwin sisters," Jim-Bob said, "and he travels all over for the hunting and the trials, but the Baldwin sisters live in an old mansion down the road, and they got kennels and everything, only there's nothing in them now."

"Wait a minute," Mr. Randolph said. "Take a breath, boy. How do you know they're real bird dog people?"

"Because in Judge Baldwin's study there's a china closet full of ribbons and cups, and over his desk there's a picture of him with a dog named Magistrate."

"Magistrate. . . ." Mr. Randolph squinted his eyes thoughtfully. "Seems to me I remember him, but it was a long time ago. Was he a black dog?"

"Yes, sir," Jim-Bob said. "And there's another black dog, lying down, in the picture."

"Lord love you, boy," Mr. Randolph said. "That other dog ain't black. I've seen other pictures like that, and one that was pretty famous a long time ago, when the two dogs up in front were Night and Joe, Jr., and the man in back was Mr. Campbell himself. The dog lying over to one side was Elcho, who was the mother of them all, and I want to tell you, boy, she wasn't black. She was *red*."

Mr. Randolph had brightened up considerably; then his face grew serious again. "You think Mr. Harry Baldwin is really looking for bird dogs like those you mentioned?"

"I know it," Jim-Bob said. "He bought a dog named Baldwin's Mary, and she was going to have puppies by the Mohawk dog, and they were going to raise them here at the Baldwin sisters'. My grandpa was going to help, if Grandma would let him, but then Baldwin's Mary got lost and never got here."

"Lost?" Mr. Randolph pulled his moustaches again. "How in tarnation does a dog get lost?"

"On a train," Jim-Bob said. "She was in a crate, and when the crate got here, she wasn't in it, and the railroad man said she probably got out and jumped off the train, but Grandma said somebody probably stole her."

"That's purely a sin and a shame," Mr. Randolph said. "It purely is."

"Shall I ask Grandpa to talk to Harry Baldwin?"

"I got to think on it," Mr. Randolph said.

He got up and walked to the cabin door, a very tall, straight old man, and looked down the road, and Nell came up and sat beside his left knee. She put her head against him, and he let his fingers touch her ear.

"You better run on home now, boy," Mr. Randolph said in a strange, weary voice. "I got some serious thinking to do."

Jim-Bob got himself untangled from the puppies and tied his shoestrings again. He stopped on the steps and turned around.

"I didn't do anything wrong, did I, sir?"

"No," Mr. Randolph said, smiling sadly at him. "You done just fine, boy. You remember that."

Jim-Bob was late for supper. He dawdled along the way, and when he got home, everyone was at the supper table, and there was nothing to do but to walk in and stand there and take his medicine.

"Where you been, son?" Olivia asked him.

"Nowhere," Jim-Bob said uncomfortably.

"What you been doing?"

Jim-Bob looked at the floor. "Nothing," he said.

John Walton put down his knife and fork and turned around. "Now, Jim-Bob," he said, "that isn't just the way I'd like to hear you answer your mother."

"Yes, sir," Jim-Bob said. He was studying the way Grandma had put the braided rug together.

It was very complicated. He thought he could recognize parts of it, like a shirt that Grandpa used to wear.

Everybody had stopped eating now and was looking at him.

"If you ask me," Grandma said, "I'd ask him where he's been spending his time the last few weeks, not just today. Seems like he's been gone every time I wanted him for something, and nobody knew where he was."

"Why, Grandma," Olivia said, "I know he hasn't been shirking his chores. He's been the first one to finish up, especially on Saturdays."

"Aha!" Grandma said conclusively. "And why do you suppose he's suddenly become so industrious, and where do you think he's gone the rest of the day?"

"Come to think of it," Olivia said, frowning, "I can't really say."

John Walton said, "Is this true, son?"

Jim-Bob found a pair of his old pants in the rug.

"Yes, sir," he said.

"I'm right sorry to hear that," John Walton said. "But I guess maybe now you better tell us what you've been doing."

Jim-Bob said nothing.

John Walton said quietly, "Son?"

Jim-Bob stopped looking at the rug and looked his father in the eye, and his father looked back at him. "I'm sorry, Daddy," he said, "I can't. I have an obligation."

"Obligation," Grandma snorted. "What does a boy like that know about obligations?"

"Just hold on there a minute, Esther," Grandpa said, and he sounded as though he meant it, so Grandma snorted again, but she didn't say any more.

"I happen to know," Grandpa said, "that Jim-Bob has a very complete understanding of obligations, because I explained it to him myself."

"Well," John Walton said, "that being the case, I think we ought to give Jim-Bob a chance to think the whole thing over, including the fact that he has some obligation to the rest of us here, just as we do to him, and then, when he's ready, maybe we can discuss it."

"I think that would be just fine," Grandpa said. "Don't you, Jim-Bob?"

"Yes, sir," Jim-Bob said.

"All right," John Walton said, picking up his knife and fork again. "Then you come over here now and have your supper. Grandma, pass Jim-Bob the mashed potatoes, please."

But it was a very quiet meal. Once Elizabeth cleared her throat to say something, but it sounded so loud that everyone looked at her, and she looked down at her plate, embarrassed.

After supper, Jim-Bob excused himself quickly and went upstairs and lay down on his bed. Presently someone else came into the room, and Jim-Bob could tell from the quiet sound of the footsteps that it was Grandpa.

"It appears to me"—Grandpa sat down on the edge of the bed—"that some of the philosophical discussions that have gone on between you and me have resulted in your getting yourself into a quandary, if not an outright dilemma."

"Do those mean trouble?" Jim-Bob's voice was somewhat muffled by the pillow.

"Invariably," Grandpa said. "Now, you said something about an obligation."

"I've got all kinds of them," Jim-Bob said into the pillow, "not even counting Reckless."

"Um, yes," Grandpa said. "That's the way it goes—feast or famine. Either a man hasn't got an obligation in the world, or he's got enough for the whole community."

Jim-Bob agreed sadly.

Grandpa said, "Before we discuss this any more, maybe I ought to tell you that Harry Baldwin is here, staying with his aunts, and he's got some posters to put up about his dog."

Jim-Bob turned over and sat up. Grandpa was taking a piece of paper out of his pocket and unfolding it. He spread it out on the bed so Jim-Bob could see it.

There was a picture of a dog, and big letters that said $100 REWARD. Jim-Bob ran his finger over the picture of the white setter with the black ears and the marks on her face. It was a picture of her on point, with her head back and her tail high, and there wasn't any doubt about it at all.

Mr. Randolph's Nell was really Baldwin's Mary.

Jim-Bob said, "Can I tell you something, Grandpa?"

"I kind of hoped you would."

"Promise not to tell?"

"Well," Grandpa said, "I reckon that might make me an accessory after the fact, which isn't so bad at my age, and considering the number of times I been accessory before the fact, and otherwise, I guess the good Lord won't mind so very much if I lay another one on him."

Jim-Bob said, "Mr. Randolph never stole her."

"I see," Grandpa said. "Mr. Randolph. How'd he get her?"

"You don't know him," Jim-Bob said, "but he said he would like to meet you one time. And I don't know how he got her, but he fixed her leg and took care of her, and he's a real good man."

"Ain't ever too many of them," Grandpa said. "Sometimes, in fact, they seem pretty scarce."

"And," Jim-Bob plunged ahead, "he pulled me out of Ketchum's pool when I would have drowned, and he took care of me, too."

"Aha!" Grandpa nodded his head. "All right, that's a genu-wine bona fidey obligation if I ever heard one."

Jim-Bob looked at Grandpa and was aware that he had a big lump in his throat.

"What am I going to do, Grandpa?"

Grandpa reached over suddenly and put his arms around Jim-Bob and gave him a big hug.

"Seems like I almost forgot how complicated growing up gets to be," he said. "Looking back, all a man remembers is fun and fishing. But you got a good start now, Jim-Bob, and you remember, a man does what he has to do, even if he don't like it much, and it either comes out right or it don't, but you've done all you can."

Jim-Bob looked at him miserably.

"Now, then," Grandpa said, "you got this obligation to Mr. Randolph."

"I gave him my word I wouldn't even mention meeting him. And I broke that already."

"Nosirree," Grandpa said. "This here is just what you call 'seeking advice from counsel,' and as your counsel, *I* can't mention it."

Jim-Bob felt better, but only a little.

"Then," Grandpa said, "you got an obligation, you might say, to society, on account of you know Baldwin's Mary is really Mr. Randolph's dog, or vice versa, but you can't say anything, because you promised Mr. Randolph you wouldn't mention meeting him."

"That's right."

"And on top of that, you got an obligation to this family to conduct yourself all aboveboard, the way you were brought up, and at the moment there's a considerable amount of doubt downstairs about how you're doing on that."

"Yes, sir," Jim-Bob said. "There—there just isn't any way out."

"Oh, pshaw," Grandpa said. "Of course there

is. Just let me think a minute."

Jim-Bob waited.

"First things first, you remember," Grandpa said. "And in this case, I'd consider the first thing is for you to go see Mr. Randolph and explain that you found out his dog is really Baldwin's Mary, if he doesn't know it."

"He doesn't know it," Jim-Bob said. "But what happens then?"

"Well," Grandpa said, "if he *does* know it, he'll probably stuff you down the well, or something, and take off into the brush. But if he's the kind of gentleman you say he is, he'll probably refer to some obligations incurred by his own upbringing, and we'll go on from there."

"I—I don't want to." Jim-Bob's lip was quivering. "You ought to see him and Nell."

"I never said there was an easy way out," Grandpa said. "Just the right way."

"I'll have to sneak out the back door. Daddy wouldn't let me go."

"Here, now," Grandpa said sternly. "That isn't the way us Waltons do things. We'll march right downstairs, explain as much as we can, and ask the family to trust us the rest of the way until we can explain the rest. Take the poster, there, along with you to show Mr. Randolph."

Downstairs, Elizabeth and Erin were listening to "The Singing Lady," and Mary Ellen was telling her father about how all the chicks were beginning to look different, and Grandma and Olivia were just finishing the dishes, but everyone turned to look at Grandpa and Jim-Bob when they came down the steps.

Grandpa cleared his throat impressively.

"Ladies and gentlemen," he said, "my client and I, here, need to take a little trip, and we ask your indulgence, because we can't tell you what it's about until it's over."

"Has this got something to do with Jim-Bob's obligation?" John Walton asked.

"Yes, sir," Jim-Bob said.

"I declare," Grandma said. "Now the old fool is talking like a lawyer."

"Counsel," Grandpa said. "Something that might not hurt most anyone I know, on certain occasions."

John Walton said, "Have you thought on this, Pa?"

"Indeed I have," Grandpa said. "In fact, we're acting on my recommendation."

"Well, then," John Walton said, "I guess the

rest of us are just going to have to go ahead and let you two do what you figure you need to and hope you'll tell us about it afterward."

"You can count on it," Grandpa said. "Shall we go, client?"

"You can't go all the way," Jim-Bob said, "on account of my word."

"That's right," Grandpa said. "I'll set in the truck and wait."

[10]

IT WAS COMING ON DARK when Jim-Bob trudged up the dusty path to the cabin. Nell heard him coming and barked, then quieted suddenly, as though Mr. Randolph had shushed her. When he came to the door and saw Jim-Bob, his face grew serious because Jim-Bob never came so late.

"What's the matter, boy?" he asked gently.

"I have to show you something," Jim-Bob said. He opened the poster and spread it out so they could see the picture on it.

Mr. Randolph looked at it for quite a while, studying the dog in the picture and somehow growing older and more tired all the time. He did not look at Nell; he didn't have to.

Presently he said, "No doubt about it, is there, boy?"

"No, sir," Jim-Bob said. "I don't guess so."

"Baldwin's Mary," Mr. Randolph said, somehow sad and proud at the same time. "Never was any doubt about her being a class dog, from the time I saw her."

Jim-Bob said in a small voice, "You didn't steal her."

"No," Mr. Randolph said, "although I suppose there'd be a question in some folks' minds."

He got up, with an effort, and took his coat down from a peg and brushed it. "Time to go, then, boy."

Jim-Bob said, "You can go across the mountain."

"That would leave you in a fine kettle of fish, wouldn't it, boy?" Mr. Randolph looked at him and smiled. "Tonight I'll go across the mountain with someone else's dog, and tomorrow the pigs will begin to fly."

"She's your dog; anybody can see that," Jim-Bob said.

"She was for a time." Mr. Randolph patted Nell's head. "And a mighty fine time it was."

"I didn't break my word," Jim-Bob said.

"I know you didn't," Mr. Randolph said. "You did just right. Now I want you to show me how to get to the Baldwins', and I'll try to do as well."

Grandpa was waiting in the truck, down beyond the first bend in the road, when they came down together, and he got out hastily when he saw them.

He and Mr. Randolph were very formal when Jim-Bob introduced them, standing out there in the road, Mr. Randolph with Nell sitting beside him. Mr. Randolph said it was a pleasant evening, and Grandpa said that was a feature of the mountains, where it cooled off nicely even in summer, and Mr. Randolph said Jim-Bob was a fine boy, and Grandpa said he could agree, but only with some qualification, considering the company. And then Grandpa said that Nell was a fine-looking dog, and Mr. Randolph said he hoped that her owner would still find her so, and he would be obliged if Grandpa could give him directions to the Baldwins' so they could find out. And, of course, Grandpa said it would be his pleasure to take the whole group over to the Baldwins' and an honor to provide a proper introduction to the ladies and Harry Baldwin, and Mr. Randolph said that was totally unnecessary, but it was more than kind, sir, and he'd be happy to take advantage of the offer. And Jim-Bob was afraid he was going to be left behind, until Grandpa opened the truck door and said, "Get in, Jim-Bob, so's you can hold the dog on your lap."

At the Baldwins', Miss Mamie opened the door, and they all went in. Miss Emily was quite fluttery when Grandpa introduced Mr. Randolph, and Miss Mamie admired the dog.

"A mighty handsome setter, Mr. Randolph," she said. "Whom does it belong to?"

"It is my belief, ma'am," Mr. Randolph said, "that she belongs to you."

"Oh, my goodness!" Miss Mamie said. "Please call Harry. He's in the study."

Harry Baldwin came out and started to be polite to Grandpa and the others, but then he saw the dog and stopped short.

"Good Lord," he said. "Is it Mary?"

Nell, or Mary, looked at him and wagged her tail slightly, as a matter of courtesy, but kept her head close to Mr. Randolph's leg.

"I believe so," Mr. Randolph said. "I found her last spring, beside the railroad tracks, on the way up from Lovingston. She had a broken leg, and I thought she'd been hit by a train and injured."

"I can't believe it!" Harry Baldwin said. "I suppose she lost the pups."

Mr. Randolph stood very straight and tall and sort of flourished his moustaches.

"It is my pleasure and great privilege, sir," he said, "to inform you that you are the owner of five splendid setter pups not twenty minutes away, by fast car."

"I need a drink," Harry Baldwin said.

Miss Mamie threw up her hands and said, "For goodness' sake, nephew."

"Oh, bother," Miss Emily said. "I think it would be most appropriate, sister, if we all had a glass of the Recipe, in celebration of this remarkable event."

While they were toasting Nell, or Mary, they strolled into the Judge's study and Mr. Randolph admired the picture of Magistrate and told Harry Baldwin about the dog in the back being Elcho. And then Mr. Randolph told about the time that Mr. Campbell put Joe, Jr., down against Gladstone in a two-day endurance race in which nothing but birds counted, because he knew that otherwise the Llewellins were going to sweep the

Campbells away, and Joe, Jr., ran Gladstone into the ground, but it really didn't help in the end. And then they talked about trials, and Mr. Randolph said he thought he'd been at most every National since the Noble pup won in '96, and the best one was probably in '09 when Alford's John, who was nine years old but maybe the smartest setter who ever lived, ran the best race of his whole life, but he happened to draw Manitoba Rap in his heat, and that was the beginning of the pointers in the National.

Then Mr. Randolph said, "I'm sorry to say, sir, that while the puppies are fine, this setter, here, is never going to run again in a field trial. The leg didn't heal just right, and she does splendidly for a little while, but I wouldn't like to see her put down for three hours against class competition, because it'd break her heart."

"I agree," Harry Baldwin said, "and it really doesn't matter that much to me. She was not a personal dog, you understand. She belonged to an old gentleman who passed away, and I was mostly interested in the puppies." He put down his glass and snapped his fingers. "And that reminds me, sir, that I'm indebted to you, and I have advertised a reward of a hundred dollars."

Mr. Randolph held up his hand sternly. "I wouldn't think of it, sir," he said. "Returning a man's dog doesn't call for anything like that. No, sir, I wouldn't think of it."

Harry Baldwin looked at Nell, or Mary, sitting close to Mr. Randolph, and then he said, "Perhaps you would keep the dog, then, since she seems attached to you, and we'll work something out with the division of her next litter."

"Done, sir," Mr. Randolph said, "on one condition: that you'll permit me to stay and help bring up those Mohawk youngsters."

"Done," Harry Baldwin said. "Now, let's go get those puppies."

Grandpa and Jim-Bob went home alone in the truck.

"Well," Grandpa said philosophically, "you see how things turn out right, once in a while. Only thing here is that I seem to have lost my autumn recreation." He turned his head and winked. "And nobody will be happier about that than your grandma."

When they got home, they saw Yancey's roadster parked out front and Sheriff Vance's big touring car with the star on the front door parked behind it.

Sheriff Vance was having a cup of coffee and saying, "Ike Godsey was telling me about the business deal that Yancey and Mary Ellen had between 'em, raising chickens, and Yancey sort of invited me out here to look at them, now that they're feathering out."

"Now, Eph," Grandpa said, "are you sure Yancey invited you?"

"Sort of," Yancey said. "It was kind of an alternative thing."

"Don't be downhearted," Grandpa said. "As far as I know, it ain't against the law to raise a flock of hens, and there ain't a rooster among 'em."

"That's terrible," Yancey said.

"I'd say it was pretty lucky," Sheriff Vance said. "You sure you ain't got a few stags tucked away somewhere?"

"No, sir," Yancey said.

"Whee!" Mary Ellen yelled suddenly. "That means they're all mine, and I can raise them."

"Dog plague it," Yancey said, "there was some good Pennsylvania stock in some of those eggs."

"Then maybe I can sell them," Mary Ellen yelled.

"Just don't do it in Jefferson County," Sheriff

Vance said, smiling at her. "As a favor to me."

Grandma could hardly keep still until they had left. Then she burst out, "I declare, I don't know what this family is coming to: pointing dogs and fighting chickens and whiskey drinking. I declare, it's all your fault, you old fool."

Grandpa said, "You forgot poker playing, old woman."

Grandma and Olivia both put their hands up to their mouths and waited for lightning or something to strike Grandpa, but John Walton slapped his hand on the table and laughed.

"After all these years, Ma, you can't tell when he's joshing you."

"The worst part," Grandma said, "is that when I think he is, he isn't."

"Fifty years," Grandpa said, "and I still got her fooled."

Suddenly there was an outcry in the yard, and everybody jumped up, because in the midst of the noise they could hear squawking, and everybody recognized Old Sairy's furious contralto.

"Oh, no!" Mary Ellen wailed. "Something's after my chickens!"

Everybody ran out of the house, shouting. The uproar was certainly around the chicken coop, and Reckless stormed out from under the porch, forgetting he was tied up, and nearly broke his neck when he reached the end of his rope. Everyone kept going, Jason bringing the lantern, except Jim-Bob. He stopped beside Reckless.

"All right," he said. "I told you I'd prove you were innocent, but now you have to help."

Reckless stood up at the end of his rope and pawed the air and roared, averring that he was ready to do battle with a Siberian tiger, if necessary to reestablish his reputation.

"Now you go get 'em," Jim-Bob said, and he untied the rope. "You sic 'em, Reckless. Hie on!"

Under ordinary circumstances, Reckless might have stopped to figure out what that last meant, but he was positive what "Sic 'em" meant, and his blood was up. He went thundering into the group around the chicken coop, and Mary Ellen began to screech, but then, after one circle, Reckless took off into the woods, baying with every jump.

"By golly," Grandpa said, "he's onto something, sure enough."

"He was the last time, too," Jim-Bob said, "if you remember when Mary Ellen's eggs were eaten, but Daddy called him back."

"Yes, sir," John Walton said, "and I'm right sorry."

He told Jason to bring the lantern, and they followed Reckless into the woods, keeping track of him by the sound. It was only a few minutes until the baying changed back to barking.

"Treed," Grandpa said. "That's what he's saying. I wonder what he's got."

"I know what he's got, Grandpa," Jim-Bob said. "He's got a fox."

And he did have. Reckless was at the foot of an old tree that leaned out over the creek, and in the lantern light, they could all see the fox crouched in a crotch about halfway up, the sharp black nose and worried face looking down at them.

John-Boy said, "Like to have a new fur collar, Mama?"

"Not at this time of year," John Walton said. "Wouldn't be much good until after frost."

"Poor thing," Olivia said, looking up. "Foxes have to live, too. I'll bet she's got a family somewhere, just waiting for a fresh chicken dinner."

The fox seemed to think about this at the same time, because it got up suddenly and ran along the trunk of the tree, jumped out into the shallow water on the far side of the creek, and disappeared in the darkness. Reckless stayed at the bottom of the tree, barking proudly.

"We might as well go in," John Walton said. "He'll never figure out that water trail."

"Daddy," Mary Ellen said, "what are we going to do about my chickens? He'll come back, won't he?"

"In another few months," Grandpa said, "that fox will have to take care of itself, if it wants to tangle with your chickens. Meanwhile, I'd suggest that we let Reckless loose again, to take care of the livestock the way he used to."

"That's a right good idea," John Walton said.

Jim-Bob said to Reckless, "There, I told you."

Reckless hung his head and wagged his tail apologetically, sorry that he'd ever doubted.

EPILOGUE
John-Boy speaking as a man

"*And thus it was, the year that Mr. Randolph, with Baldwin's Mary, came to Walton's Mountain and changed life for Jim-Bob so that he was never quite the same afterward. For that was the year that he learned a long journey begins with the first short step, and we all learned with him that the first step may be the hardest one of all.*

"*Mr. Randolph and the dogs moved on, in time, to what future glories I do not remember, but surely they were deserved, and the lessons of style and courage they left behind stayed with Jim-Bob, and with us all, in later years. That was a good summer, among many for us there, because so many things turned out so well for so many of us, and even for Yancey and Reckless, it had to be termed a good summer on balance, considering the alternatives.*"